Praise for *Brightwood*

"A proper page-turning thriller."

—*The Guardian*

"Think of it as *Home Alone* meets *Coraline*—the perfect spine-tingler for 9- to 12-year-old readers."

—*Richmond Times-Dispatch*

"Brilliantly conceived . . . Subtle and thought-provoking, the novel is entertaining and heartfelt."

—*Kirkus Reviews*

"This is the best kind of middle-grade thriller: atmospheric with just the right amount of scare and a few bits of humor as a bonus . . . Readers who loved Beatty's mansion-set *Serafina and the Black Cloak* will happily wander Brightwood's grounds and explore its mysteries."

—*Bulletin of the Center for Children's Books*

"Filled with action and intrigue . . . This suspenseful story will keep intrepid readers transfixed."

—*The Horn Book Magazine*

"Compelling and mesmerizing, *Brightwood* is a dazzling middle grades read sure to captivate! *Brightwood* is everything a story should be . . . Highly, highly recommended for all middle grades and anyone who gets lost in a great story."

—**Pamela Thompson, reviewer for the** *El Paso Times*

"A nice read-alike for fans of Jonathan Auxier's *The Night Gardener* or Neil Gaiman's *Coraline*."

—*School Library Journal*

"Beautiful, evocative writing brings Daisy's world to life, and readers will empathize with Daisy and admire her courage and resourcefulness."
—*Booklist*

"Thrilling and dark, this novel will leave tween readers asking themselves where imagination ends and madness begins."
—AMightyGirl.com

"*Brightwood* is a fast-paced, exhilarating novel that keeps readers on their toes: terrified, entranced, angered and in love with the characters Unsworth creates."
—CenteredonBooks.com

"Unsworth's beautiful and haunting descriptions bring Brightwood Hall to life and draw readers into Daisy's world. Young readers will be rooting for Daisy as she prepares to fight for her home and flee if necessary in this entrancing story that will keep everyone guessing till the very end."
—*BNKIDS* blog

"Tania Unsworth's *Brightwood* is like a fancifully crafted keepsake box from another era containing a perfectly contemporary sensibility. It's intrepid in exploring feelings of abandonment, orphanhood, peril and loss. Its new brand of magic is just right for today."
—CenterforFiction.org

"Dive deep into the mysterious circumstances that besiege Brightwood . . . Adventure awaits readers around every bend . . . A charming read."
—*Independent Voice* (Dixon, CA)

"Frighteningly beautiful."
—*From the Mixed-Up Files . . . of Middle-Grade Authors* blog

BRIGHTWOOD

ALSO BY TANIA UNSWORTH

The One Safe Place

BRIGHTWOOD

Tania Unsworth

ALGONQUIN YOUNG READERS 2018

Published by
Algonquin Young Readers
an imprint of Algonquin Books of Chapel Hill
Post Office Box 2225
Chapel Hill, North Carolina 27515-2225

a division of
Workman Publishing
225 Varick Street
New York, New York 10014

First paperback edition, Algonquin Young Readers, April 2018.
Originally published in hardcover by Algonquin Young Readers,
September 2016.
Printed in the United States of America.
Published simultaneously in Canada by Thomas Allen & Son Limited.
Design by Carla Weise.

LIBRARY OF CONGRESS CATALOGING-IN-PUBLICATION DATA
Names: Unsworth, Tania, author.
Title: Brightwood / Tania Unsworth.
Description: First edition. | Chapel Hill, North Carolina :
Algonquin Young Readers, 2016. | Summary: When her mother disappears and
a menacing stranger tries to claim her home, Brightwood Hall, for himself, Daisy
must use her wits, courage, and help from her imaginary friends to survive.
Identifiers: LCCN 2016017356 | ISBN 9781616203306 (HC)
Subjects: | CYAC: Dwellings—Fiction. | Imaginary playmates—Fiction. |
Survival—Fiction. | Mothers and daughters—Fiction.
Classification: LCC PZ7.U44178 Br 2016 | DDC [Fic]—dc23
LC record available at https://lccn.loc.gov/2016017356

ISBN 978-1-61620-748-9 (PB)

10 9 8 7 6 5 4 3 2 1
First Paperback Edition

For Moony and Little Ma,
Then and always.

BRIGHTWOOD

THIRTY YEARS AGO

The yacht was as grand and as white as a wedding cake and it was named *Everlasting*. Every inch of it had been polished, from the great, gleaming hull down to the last brass button on the uniform of the three crewmen standing in line on deck. The anchor had been lifted and the vessel was ready for departure. But first there was a picture to be taken.

When you are as rich and as good-looking as the Fitzjohn family was, there is always someone who wants to take your picture.

The photographer from the society pages of the newspaper had arranged the Fitzjohns on the dock with their yacht in the background. Or rather, he had *suggested* they pose that way, his smile ingratiating because after all, it was they who were doing him the favor.

There they stood under the bluest of all blue skies. Mrs. Fitzjohn, her lovely face smiling under a large-brimmed, fashionable hat, and Mr. Fitzjohn, tanned and gallant in his navy blazer, gazing fondly at his wife. In front of them, their children, Marcus and Caroline. At seventeen, Marcus was almost as tall as his father and just as handsome. Caroline was six. She was holding a doll. The doll was also called Caroline. It had been handmade in Switzerland especially for her. It had the same color hair and eyes as her and was wearing the same yellow cotton dress that Caroline herself was wearing.

"Wonderful . . . lovely . . . " the photographer said automatically as he fiddled with his camera. "Won't take a minute!" But then he looked—really *looked*—at them and the breath suddenly caught in his throat.

It seemed that the Fitzjohns were shining almost as brightly as the sunlight on the water of the bay. It wasn't just their wealth, the fact that along with the fabulous yacht, they owned a fleet of cars and a beautiful mansion called Brightwood Hall. Nor was it merely their good looks and glamour. Plenty of celebrities had these qualities, as he well knew.

No, he thought. It was happiness they shone with. The photographer had witnessed too many fake smiles and phony jollity not to recognize the real thing when he saw it. In that moment—that perfect moment—he thought the Fitzjohns looked like the happiest people in the entire world.

He sighed. The camera clicked.

"All done, Mr. Fitzjohn! Hope you have a great day on the water!"

Caroline Fitzjohn trotted after the others as they went on board. Daddy and Marcus would go straight to the pilot's deck like they always did, but Mummy had said there were cookies for her in the main cabin.

"We shall have tea!" she had said. "You and I and Dolly Caroline. Would you like that?"

Caroline thought she would like it very much, but now Mummy had disappeared somewhere. Perhaps she had gone to the pilot's deck after all, or perhaps she was in the bathroom.

Caroline stood in the main cabin waiting for her mother to come back and feeling lonely. But of course she wasn't really alone. She had Dolly Caroline with her. She stroked the doll's hair and straightened her dress.

"Oh, *Caroline*," she said out loud. "You lost your shoe!"

For a moment, she thought of calling out to her mother. Then she remembered that she was six years old. Six was old enough to look after her own things. Besides, she'd already realized where the shoe must have fallen off. She had been playing on a little bench by the dock, making Dolly Caroline walk up and down the wooden seat while the others got ready for the trip. The bench wasn't far away. She could see it through the cabin window.

It took only a minute to slip off the boat and run down the gangplank. And then she was on her hands and knees looking under the bench for the shoe. She couldn't see it anywhere and then there it was, a scrap of yellow leather wedged between the wall and the back of the bench. Caroline climbed onto the seat and reached down as far as her arm would go. She could feel the shoe! She scissored her fingers and tried to snag it, fearful that she would wedge it down even more. But she had a grip on it now, one finger hooked in the tiny laces. She was pulling it to safety.

Something made her look up. A premonition.

For a second, she saw only the empty space where the *Everlasting* had been. Then her gaze lifted and she saw the yacht out in the bay. It was moving fast; there was white water behind it, and the flag on its topmost mast was flattened to a sheet. Caroline ran to the edge of the dock.

The yacht was flying away. Two hundred yards, now three. She held Dolly Caroline tight to her chest and watched it go.

They had left without her. They hadn't known.

The driver, Mr. Hadley, came to pick her up. Her grandmother, who had stayed behind at home, would look after her for the day. Her family would be back that afternoon. It was only a day trip, so she wouldn't have missed much. Someone would radio the yacht to tell them she was safe. Mr. Hadley explained all this in a kind voice as he drove the twenty or so miles back to Brightwood Hall.

Caroline sat in the back of the big car, gazing out the window. She had always loved the sea but now it suddenly seemed a featureless, unfriendly place. And there, far away, in the middle of the emptiness, looking no larger than a glittering brooch pinned to the very edge of the horizon, she saw the *Everlasting*. She pressed her hand to the window, staring desperately. There was a bend in the road and then the yacht was gone.

"You'll take plenty of other trips," Mr. Hadley said. His voice was kinder than ever. "It's still only the start of summer."

But there were no more trips.

Mummy and Daddy and Marcus didn't come back in the afternoon, and although Caroline sat at the top of the great staircase, waiting for them, they kept not coming back. The shadows on the marble floor of the hallway below stretched farther and farther away. The phone rang. She heard her grandmother's voice. "Hello?" and a long silence. Then there was a knock at the door, and suddenly the hallway was filled with people in dark blue uniforms. Caroline couldn't hear what they were talking about. Her grandmother was clutching the front of her white ruffled shirt, pulling it tighter and tighter. Across the hallway, she saw Maggie, the housekeeper. Maggie was a stout, dignified woman who didn't look as if she had ever run in her life. Now she was running.

Somebody made a wailing sound and Caroline heard crying from the kitchen.

Her cousin, James, who was staying with them for the summer, like he always did, came down the corridor behind her. He had been in his room all day, feeling ill.

"I don't know what's happening," Caroline said, her voice trembling. "What's happening?"

But James walked straight past her.

Later, Caroline's grandmother sat with her on the sofa in the blue drawing room and told her that Mummy and Daddy and Marcus were never coming back. And the three crew members who had been working on the *Everlasting* weren't coming back either. There had been an accident, a terrible accident.

Caroline found it hard to make out exactly what her grandmother was saying. Her voice was so whispery and she kept breaking off to cry, and kiss Caroline, and press Caroline's face against her ruffled shirt.

It wasn't until the next day that she fully understood what had happened. Someone had left a copy of the newspaper lying on the table by the front door. The photographer's picture had been made large and filled almost the whole of the front page. There were words above it, written in thick black letters almost as big as Caroline's hand:

TRAGEDY AT SEA—

FITZJOHN FAMILY LOST!

The massive explosion yesterday on board the Fitzjohn family yacht is believed to have been caused by engine failure. There are no survivors.

And there they all were: Mummy and Daddy and Marcus and herself. And there was the *Everlasting* with her crew on deck. And there too was Dolly Caroline—she could see clearly because the picture was so big—wearing only one little yellow shoe.

That afternoon, Caroline felt strangely restless. She left her grandmother's side and wandered around the house by herself, collecting things. She didn't know why she did it, only that she felt she must. On the floor in the blue drawing room, she found her grandmother's handkerchief. It was pale pink and covered with dark smudges that Caroline thought might be makeup. She picked it up and put it in her pocket. In the kitchen, she tore off the top from the box of cereal she'd had for breakfast and put that in her pocket as well. She added a pretty plastic bracelet that she happened to be wearing. Then she went to her bedroom, fetched an empty shoe box from her closet, and placed all the items inside.

Last, she took Dolly Caroline off her bed and put her in the box, arranging her carefully so that her hair wouldn't get mussed. She put the lid on the box and slid it underneath her bed, where it was dark and safe.

Caroline Fitzjohn had decided that she was never going to lose anything ever again.

DAY ONE

ONE

It wasn't the screaming—it was the sound of the car in the driveway that woke her up.

Daisy was used to the screaming. It came from the peacocks that had gone wild years ago. They always made a lot of noise just before dawn.

She sat up, confused. Her mum hadn't told her she was going out. She always went to the bulk-buy store on Wednesday but today was Monday. Her mum had described the place to Daisy, the size of it and how it was crammed from floor to ceiling with provisions. Daisy thought it sounded a lot like their basement here at Brightwood Hall.

Daisy listened as the sound of the car grew fainter and fainter and then disappeared. She curled back under the covers and closed her eyes. Wherever she was going, her mum would be back by eleven o'clock. She was never late.

When Daisy woke up again, the sun was high in the sky. Daisy's bedroom was on the second floor, at the front west corner of the main house. One window gave her a view of the lake and the grounds on the western side. From the other, she could see a good part of the front of the house, including the stone balcony above the main entrance and the two urns—one that had fallen over, one still on its pedestal—to her left and right. Beyond the entrance was the long stretch of driveway. It was gravel, although the gravel was mottled with patches of weed and grass. From this distance, Daisy thought the driveway looked as if it were covered with fur. Like the speckled coat of a great snow leopard, wrapped around the house.

The driveway curved away across the lawn towards the entrance gates a quarter of a mile away. But *lawn* was the wrong word for it. Daisy and her mum could manage to keep the grass short only close to the house. The rest of it was more like a meadow, waist high in places and dense with wildflowers. It spread almost all the way to the perimeter wall, interrupted by huge trees—oak and cedar—their trunks hidden in green shadow. The trees grew thicker down near the front gates, so thick you couldn't see the road beyond, only the distant hills and the tiny spike of a church tower. Behind the hills, hidden from view, lay the ocean.

Daisy put on a T-shirt and shorts and went to get some breakfast. Directly outside her room was the Portrait Gallery, with pictures hanging on the wall on one side and a wooden banister on the other, with a view of the Marble Hall below. You could see only the tops of some pictures, while others—such as the painting of the General and the one of the Lady on Horseback— were clearly visible. Most, however, were hidden behind tall piles of books stacked on the floor.

Daisy stood on her tiptoes and looked at Little Charles through a gap between two piles of books. He was a recent discovery. Up until now, the only person in the Portrait Gallery that Daisy had spoken with was the Lady on Horseback. But the Lady was far too fierce and full of herself to spend time in idle chat, and it was a relief when Daisy found Little Charles instead. Not that there was much of him to see, just the top half of his body. His dark hair was cut in the shape of a pudding bowl, and there was a frilly white collar around his neck.

"Hey," she said softly.

"Good morning," Little Charles said.

"You okay?"

"Certainly not!" Little Charles said. "It's fearfully cramped in here."

Daisy moved the books carefully, widening the gap. The rest of Little Charles's body came into view.

"Oh!" Daisy cried. "You're wearing a dress!"

"I am *not*! My mother wears dresses. This is a *tunic*." He sounded extremely cross. "I could have you whipped for saying that."

"Well, you might have been able to in the olden days, but you can't now," Daisy said, pushing the books some more. Little Charles's hand appeared, clutching a wooden hoop.

"So that's what I've been holding on to!" he exclaimed. "I thought it was the back of a chair. My hoop! Isn't it the most marvelous thing?"

"It's lovely," she said, not wanting to hurt his feelings.

"I *may* let you borrow it," Little Charles said, a cunning note entering his voice. "If you made more space, I would. For sure."

"I'll try later," Daisy said. "I have to get breakfast now."

She walked past the General. She had always been frightened of his long, curled mustache and pale eyes, and over time, her fear had grown until she couldn't even look at him. Partly it was because the General had The Crazy. Her mum had told her that The Crazy wasn't something you could catch, but even so, it was best to be on the safe side. Daisy hurried along, averting her eyes.

At the top of the stairs, she paused. The grand staircase at Brightwood Hall was made of white marble, and it fanned out as it descended, like the train of an evening gown. A strip of blue-velvet carpet ran down the middle of the stairs, which were kept free of all obstruction. Below, in the Marble Hall, it was different. The vast space was crowded from wall to wall with shelving units, all placed close together, forming a kind of maze. The units were more than twenty feet tall and filled with thousands and thousands of boxes, and the paths between them were extremely narrow. Even Daisy's mum, who was slim, had to turn sideways to make her way through.

Daisy didn't need to do that because she could climb so well. Although she was frightened of a great many things—storms, the dark, the picture of the General, the groaning noise the water pipes made when the weather grew cold—she had never been afraid to climb. She climbed like a monkey. Not quite as well as a monkey, perhaps, because she didn't have a tail, but almost as well because she didn't have to think about it. She swung herself up the nearest shelving unit and scuttled on hands and knees across the top shelf. At eleven years old, she was getting bigger and heavier, but there wasn't any danger of the shelves collapsing. They were made of steel and bolted to the floor.

When she got to the edge of the shelf, she leaped across to the next one, her braid bouncing against her back. Daisy's hair was long and thick and black. Her mum had the same hair; only hers was a beautiful silver color. Apart from that, they didn't look alike at all. Daisy's mum was tall and long limbed and graceful. She moved slowly, as if she were afraid she might break. But Daisy was quick, her body strong and compact.

In the evenings, she undid her braid and her hair hung shining down to her waist. "You must never cut it," her mum often said as she brushed it. "It would break my heart."

Daisy's mum didn't like things to change. When one of the old cedar trees fell down in a storm the previous winter, she had cried for a whole afternoon.

Daisy jumped to the next shelf. Below her, in the center of the hall, there was a clearing amidst the ranks of shelves, right beneath the chandelier. She half ran, half crawled until she was close enough to the chandelier to touch it. It was the size of her mum's four-poster bed, and it had been installed when Brightwood Hall had been built, over two hundred and fifty years ago. It hung from a thick chain that looped around the wheel of a pulley attached to the ceiling and then curved away in a long line to another pulley bolted to the wall on the far side. Somewhere behind one of the shelving units, there was a handle you could turn to lower the chandelier to the ground to make repairs or to clean it. But it hadn't been cleaned in a long while, and its light, once dazzlingly brilliant, had softened behind a veil of dust.

Daisy never passed the chandelier without marveling at its beauty. If the corridors were the arteries of the house and the walls were its bones and the ivy on the outside was its skin, then the chandelier was the heart of Brightwood Hall. It was both terribly heavy and terribly fragile, and it was made of ten thousand crystal tears.

She jumped from shelf to shelf until she reached the far-left corner of the hall, then she slipped to the ground and went down the passage along one side of the ballroom, squeezing through the gap between piled-up boxes, until she reached the kitchen at the back of the house. It wasn't Brightwood Hall's main kitchen, which had become full a while ago. It was a much smaller room, which her mum called "the old servants' kitchen." Daisy had always wondered why old servants needed a special kitchen, although she never asked.

There were a lot of things she wondered about but didn't ask.

Daisy liked the kitchen because you could move around in it easily. Her mum didn't keep anything in there unless it was needed to make or eat food. She was strict about that. It was the same in the bathrooms, which her mum insisted on keeping perfectly clean and empty.

Daisy fetched a bowl of cereal, whistling for Tar. The minute she dipped her spoon, he scampered up the table leg to join her, staring at the bowl expectantly, his oily eyes shining. Daisy waved him away.

"Wait on the floor. Just because our house is cluttered, it

doesn't mean it's dirty," Daisy told him, repeating something her mum often said. "You shouldn't be on the table."

Tar blinked rapidly a few times. "There's six stages of dirty in the world," he began. He was fond of making lists.

"First there's *grimy*. Not much to grimy, just dust and skin cells and the like. Next up is *grubby*—stains and smudges, that sort of thing. One stage further, and now you're talking *greasy*, closely followed by *grotty*, which is a nice, rich stage, layers of filth one on top of the other . . . "

Daisy was only half listening. She was thinking that Tar was one of her better names, not only because Tar was completely black, but also because it was *rat* spelled backwards. He sat up on his hind legs with his paws clasped eagerly together.

"After *grotty* comes *gross*, a stage of dirty that's hard to come by. Takes years of development. True grossness is a thing of wonder."

"What's the sixth stage?" Daisy asked.

Tar's eyes closed for a second. His paws became still.

"Gagging," he said in a hushed voice. "Only experienced it once in my life. I was a young rat. My mum took me down to the sewers as part of my education." He paused and drew in his breath. "Who knew there were such things in the world?"

"If you liked it so much, why don't you go back there?"

"Something, something, something," Tar mumbled. He

always said that when he wouldn't—or couldn't—answer a question.

Daisy washed her spoon and bowl and wiped down the kitchen surfaces and put the box of cereal back in the cupboard. It was the last box there, so she went down to the basement and got another two boxes and noted in the log that there were now only nineteen left in the stores. It was nearly ten o'clock.

Daisy knew she should start her schoolwork, although she didn't want to. She decided to delay it by feeding the animals. She fetched some leftover lettuce, half a loaf of stale-ish bread, and a bag of birdseed, and slipped out of the kitchen into the sunshine. A lot of animals lived in the grounds of Brightwood Hall. Along with a multitude of birds, there were rabbits and hedgehogs and field mice and squirrels and a red fox that could be seen sometimes in the early morning, trotting down the overgrown pathways, its coat glistening with dew. Daisy loved them all and rarely went outside without a pair of binoculars around her neck to keep track of them.

She made her way to her favorite spot next to the glasshouse and spread the lettuce on the ground. It was early June and the animals could easily find their own food, but she never grew tired of seeing them. Sometimes the rabbits came so close they almost took the lettuce out of her hand.

Today, however, they didn't seem interested. Daisy scattered the birdseed and bread, and was instantly surrounded by a flurry of wings and darting beaks. It was mostly sparrows and starlings this morning, although she noticed a couple of blackbirds among the throng. She flung the food in smaller and smaller handfuls until it was all gone.

"Don't fly away," she told the birds.

But they were off the instant the last crumb was eaten.

Her mum would be home soon. Daisy thought if she walked down the driveway to the front gates, she would probably meet her. She made her way back through the house to fetch the little wagon they used to pick up deliveries. When Daisy had been younger, too young to be left alone in the house, her mum had ordered everything using her phone, and there had been deliveries every single day. Now her mum went out to shop, but sometimes she bought too much to fit in the car and the rest had to be delivered. There was often a pile of boxes waiting by the gates.

Brightwood Hall was so large and it was so difficult—even for Daisy—to get around in it that it was almost a quarter to eleven before she got to the front entrance where the wagon was kept. She glanced up at the picture by the door. Her mum had painted it. She painted nearly every day, although she never seemed pleased by her work.

"It's wrong," she would say after finishing each painting. "I haven't *caught* it."

Daisy didn't know what her mum was trying to catch. She thought the paintings were wonderful. But her mum kept all of them in her bedroom, stacked up with their faces to the wall.

This was the only exception. It was a portrait of Daisy sitting in the meadow, with her lap full of flowers. Behind her was Brightwood Hall, with all its chimneys and decorative details outlined against the sky. The painting wasn't completely realistic, because her mum had painted the ocean in the distance even though you couldn't see it from the house in real life. A tiny glittering boat floated on the far horizon. If you peered hard enough, you could see something written on the side of it.

The *Everlasting*.

The word gave Daisy a strange, sad feeling. Her mum had lost almost her whole family in an accident on that boat.

But that was long ago. And her mum didn't think about it much, because she hardly every mentioned it. Daisy turned her gaze to her mum's signature at the bottom of the painting: *Caroline Fitzjohn*.

She would be home soon, Daisy thought as she went out the front door, pulling the wagon behind her. All the way down the drive, she expected to see her mum coming back, the big blue car loaded up with boxes of laundry soap and kitchen towels and tubs of coffee, with the little toy kitten that hung from the rearview mirror swaying to and fro. When Daisy was small, that tiny plush kitten, with its gray fur and blue eyes, was her favorite toy. One day, in a fit of generosity, she'd wrapped it up in a bit of leftover Christmas wrapping paper and given it to her mum. Her mum hadn't asked her whether she was sure she wanted to part with it. But her mum knew the gift was a big deal. She had tied a blue ribbon around the kitten's waist and hung it from the mirror in her car. It always made Daisy smile to see the kitten as her mum's car came up the bumpy driveway towards the house.

There was no car today. Just the path and then the tall gates surrounded by trees. The gates were so finely wrought and so elaborately designed, they looked like sheets of lace. But they were made of iron and extremely strong. Tall pedestals stood on either side, with a stone lion on the top of each one. The lion on the left was called Regal and the one on the right was Royal. When they had been new, they had been identical, although time and the weather had changed their expressions. Now Regal appeared stern, almost angry. And there were dark markings on Royal's cheeks that looked like tears.

The lions always said the same thing.

"Beware!" Regal warned.

"Be careful!" Royal wept.

Daisy rested her hand on the padlock that held the gates shut and stared out into the road beyond. There was nothing to see. She didn't open the gates and go outside because she wasn't allowed to. She was never allowed to.

She had been born in one of the dozens of bedrooms in Brightwood Hall. And in the whole of her life, she had never once set foot outside.

TWO

There were two worlds in Daisy's life. There was the outside world and there was the world of Brightwood Hall. And only Brightwood Hall, with its labyrinth of rooms, its many animals, its ancient trees and secret corners, seemed quite real to her.

She could see the outside world. But it felt like a faraway place. Daisy knew there were towns and cities out there, rivers and mountains, millions of people living their lives, although she knew about them only from pictures in books and in stories she had read. She was curious, of course, and the older she got, the more questions she had. But the answers to the questions seemed as unreal as the outside world itself. Brightwood Hall was the only place she had ever known or felt a part of. And now she stood at its gates, staring out like a fish in a pond might stare at the strange and distant bank.

She turned at last and started back towards the house.

Maybe Mum forgot something at the store and had to go back.

It was an obvious explanation. Her mum couldn't call the house and tell her because she didn't have a phone anymore. She had stopped using it about three years ago, around the same time that she got rid of the television. Daisy had been sorry when the television went. She had watched cartoons on it and shows about wild animals. Then her mum said they didn't need it any longer.

"It's easy to waste far too much time with things like that," her mum had said. "Television, phones, computers . . . "

"What are computers?" Daisy wanted to know.

Her mum didn't seem to hear the question. "People spend almost their whole lives looking at screens. They turn into strangers, like zombies."

Daisy thought this sounded frightening, although she still didn't know what it had to do with shows about wild animals. She didn't ask. Her mum looked away, her eyes distant, and Daisy could tell she didn't want to talk about it anymore.

She decided to get on with her schoolwork until her mum came back. Daisy wriggled and climbed her way across the Marble Hall and went into the ballroom. It was the second largest room in Brightwood Hall, and it was crammed wall to wall with furniture that had been removed from the rest of the house to make space. Ornate plaster decorations covered the ceiling, and the sunlight fell in stripes through tall windows. You could see most of the eastern side of the grounds of Brightwood Hall from here: the walled gardens, the topiary, and a stretch of the Wilderness.

The furniture in the ballroom was covered with white dust-covers. Daisy thought the covers made everything look like a picture she had once seen of the Arctic. If she squinted, she could imagine that the tables and chairs were snowy peaks with long valleys, full of shadow.

The only thing not covered was a desk by the window. Daisy sat down and gathered up her books.

It was Monday, which meant she had history and then math, followed by English. Her mum taught her all the subjects and was very organized about it. They used books from the house's huge library. At the moment, they were learning about the Romans. Daisy liked the Romans. Their buildings reminded her of Brightwood Hall, with its four great columns at the entrance and the triangular pediment set high up on the front. She turned to the next chapter, which was all about gladiators, and spent half an hour reading and taking notes.

She wasn't nearly so interested in math. She opened the

textbook unwillingly and forced herself to concentrate. It was algebra. Her mum said most kids didn't study that until they were twelve or older, although that didn't mean much to Daisy. The whole idea of kids her age was a bit like algebra itself: hard to keep straight because there was nothing real attached to it. She sighed and tapped her pencil against the page.

Her mum usually helped her with the harder problems. Daisy glanced at her watch. It was nearly one o'clock.

Maybe she got a flat tire and had to wait for it to be fixed.

Daisy abandoned the last few problems and moved on to English. They were reading *Macbeth* by somebody named William Shakespeare. The words were hard and Daisy often felt confused. Normally, her mum spoke the lines out loud, explaining what the words meant as she went along. Sometimes she got up from her chair on the other side of the desk and paced slowly among the white shrouded furniture, her hands gesturing and her voice full of feeling.

But her mum wasn't here. Daisy stared hard at the page.

"Confusion now hath made his . . . masterpiece," she ventured, her voice coming out in a whisper. *"Most sac . . . sac . . . sacrilegious . . ."*

The clock in the distant drawing room chimed. It was half past one already. She had heard the sound ten thousand times, but it had a different voice today. As if it were calling to remind her of the quietness of the house and how alone she was.

She considered going into the kitchen to see if Tar was around. He had been particularly talky that morning. That was because her mum wasn't there. Her mum didn't like it when she talked to animals and objects, although she had liked it when Daisy was small.

"What an imagination you have!" she used to say when Daisy gave the hedgehogs names or had a long conversation with a tree or with one of the many statues that dotted the grounds of Brightwood Hall. Daisy preferred talking to these things rather than to her dolls, all of whom were rather dull.

"All they do is drink tea and argue about who has the nicest hair," she complained. "And the biggest one, Janice, is so bossy. She thinks she's better than the others because she's the only one who's still got her knickers."

Her mum had laughed out loud. "It's amazing how you bring things to life!"

Daisy hadn't thought she brought things to life. She'd thought everything was already alive. Not just plants and animals, but also twigs and pebbles and stars and every last one of her toys.

A part of her still thought the same way. That everything had a secret life of its own, with its own thoughts and feelings. It was as if there were a gap—perhaps as narrow as a crack in the path or as wide as the meadow itself—between what was real and what was not.

Her mum used to like her talking to things, but not any longer. Now it seemed to worry her.

Daisy turned her gaze to the many photographs and portraits that hung from the walls of the ballroom. They were mostly pictures of former Fitzjohns. Many had been great men and women in their time. There was Emily Fitzjohn, the famous campaigner for women's rights, and Talbot Fitzjohn, who had been ambassador to China, and Harry Herbert Fitzjohn, a champion swimmer. Daisy's favorite was the celebrated explorer Sir Clarence Fitzjohn, who had lived a hundred and fifty years ago. He had been knighted after his daring attempt to travel around the world in a hot-air balloon. The picture of Sir Clarence was in black and white. He was wearing a strangely shaped helmet and standing with one foot on the head of a tiger that he had just shot. Sir Clarence had mounted expeditions to the North Pole, Mount Everest, and Papua New Guinea, but he had spent most of his life searching the Amazon for the Lost City of Valcadia, which was said to be made entirely of silver. Nobody knew if Sir Clarence ever found the city, because he disappeared somewhere in the jungles of Brazil and was never heard from again.

Not all the Fitzjohns had been as admirable as Sir Clarence.

One had been hung for murder and another had been an infamous traitor. Several had been notorious for their cruelty. Like the General, they all had The Crazy.

"It runs through our family," Daisy's mum had explained.

"What is it?" Daisy wanted to know.

Her mum shook her head. "I don't know for sure," she said. "The people who have it are born different . . . wrong."

"Don't worry," she'd added, seeing Daisy's anxious face. "It hasn't appeared for a long, long time."

Daisy closed her book and placed it back on the desk. There was no point trying to go on with her schoolwork. She was far too distracted.

Maybe Mum felt sleepy, so she stopped for a nap.

But this explanation, like all the others, suddenly seemed thin and unconvincing. For the first time, Daisy wondered whether something else had happened to her mother.

Something bad.

THREE

Daisy thought the best thing to do was to act as if nothing were wrong. If she treated the day as if it were perfectly normal, perhaps the day would realize it had made a mistake and go back to *being* normal.

In the afternoon, her mum usually set up her easel to paint, and Daisy played or worked on one of her animal projects. At the moment, she was studying the peacocks. When her mum had been a little girl, the peacocks of Brightwood Hall had been three pairs of standard Indian blues. Now there were more than a hundred birds and they were all different: blue blotched, black barred, mixtures of silver, bronze, and green. One was completely white with an emerald crest, another brown and drab looking except for a cloak of gold over its shoulders. They lived in the Wilderness, a huge overgrown expanse on the northern side of the estate.

Daisy fetched her notebook and went down the path by the west wing, with the lake on her left and the statue of the Hunter directly ahead of her in a little circle where the path widened. She stopped when she got to him and reached up to touch his foot. The Hunter stared into the distance with one arm flung out and the other at his shoulder, reaching for his bow. He was leaning forward, one leg bent, the other lifted, as if he had just at that moment broken into a run. His face was smooth and beautiful.

"What do you see today?" Daisy asked him.

"Far horizons," the Hunter said. "Strange shores."

It was difficult getting any real information out of the Hunter because he was so poetic.

"When you say 'strange,'" Daisy attempted, "do you mean strange as in weird, or do you just mean strange as in new to you? And where are you looking?"

"Forward, ever forward, beyond the mists of time . . . "

Daisy felt a bit sorry for the Hunter. He could never say anything directly. He could speak only in the grandest and most complicated language.

She carried on down the path and then through the bushes that fringed the Wilderness, retracing a route where the undergrowth had been pushed aside. There was a clearing where the peacocks liked to roost, high in the trees. Daisy sat down with her back against a tree trunk and made herself as still as she could.

In a little while, three of the birds made their way into the clearing: two females, pecking and peering, and a male with a greenish breast and white crest. Daisy made a note of the time and place in her book and then a description of their coloring.

For all their glory, they were lazy creatures. Their nests were just little holes they scraped in the earth, and they would rather run than fly. The fattest ones got eaten by the fox.

Daisy liked this area of the Wilderness because the Christmas tree was there. She glanced across at it now. The tree had grown faster than her. It was already twice her height. Last year, even her mum wasn't tall enough to fix the star on the top without a ladder. When the tree was decorated, it was a beautiful sight, all lit up among the dark trees. They scattered grain and dried fruit for the animals, and hung balls of seed so that birds would come and perch among the branches, as if they were Christmas decorations themselves.

"Are we the only people who have a Christmas tree?" Daisy had once asked.

"Oh no. Lots of people get them to put in the house."

"The *house*? How do the animals get their treats?"

Her mum had smiled at that and squeezed her hand.

Back then, she could talk to her mum about anything. Her mum told her stories about when she was a little girl, when Brightwood Hall was full of people and laughter. The meadow was still a lawn then, the grass kept short by a dozen gardeners, and the Wilderness was a well-tended woodland, covered by bluebells in the spring.

In those days, her mum slept in a bedroom with a garden painted on the walls, and the rest of the house was equally beautiful. The Fitzjohn silver was always polished and the windows gleamed. There were parties, her mum said. Such parties! The women wore dresses all the way down to the ground and danced through the night in the ballroom.

"Where did they put all the covered-up furniture?"

"It wasn't there. The ballroom was perfectly empty."

"Did you wear a long dress? Did you dance too?"

"I wasn't allowed to stay up so late . . . "

But now that Daisy was older, her mum didn't seem to like her asking so many questions. Sometimes when Daisy was talking, her mum's face would change, and if Daisy didn't stop, she would start to run the heel of her slender hand against her forehead, over and over again. And whatever Daisy was talking about would lose all meaning, as if her mum were rubbing the words away.

It was much easier to keep quiet and talk instead to Little Charles or Tar or the peacocks.

FOUR

It was long past lunchtime. But although Daisy was hungry, she walked back to the house as slowly as she could. The slower she walked, the longer she could hope that her mum had come back while Daisy had been in the Wilderness. On the way, she bargained.

If she's back, I will never say anything that will make her rub her forehead. I will brush my teeth every day and not lie that I did it. I will stop picking the paint off the wall behind my bed . . .

She went in by the front door, crossed the reception area—stacked high with unopened deliveries—and entered the Marble Hall.

"Mum?"

Daisy made her voice louder. *"Mum!"*

Nothing answered, not even an echo. She stood still for a second and then suddenly plunged into the maze of shelving, running as fast as she could up and down the narrow lanes, turning left and right, her eyes wide with searching, as if she could find her mum if only she looked hard enough. She stopped at last and pulled herself together.

She should make lunch. Lunch was normal.

Daisy went into the kitchen. She had been teaching herself to cook using recipe books from the library. Her mum never got into the habit of cooking because she had always had people to make her meals when she was growing up. Daisy, however, enjoyed it. The basement at Brightwood Hall was stocked with thousands and thousands of items, and she could always find the ingredients she needed. But today she wasn't in the mood. She made herself a cheese sandwich.

Tar was sitting on the table, waiting for her.

"You should be careful," Daisy told him. "Mum only lets me keep you because you're not a wild rat. You look like you used to be someone's pet. If she sees you on the table, she might change her mind. She told me rats shouldn't be in the house at all. People put down traps and poison for them."

Tar's gaze was nailed to the sandwich. "I'd never fall for that," he said.

Daisy waved the sandwich slowly to and fro in front of him. "Are you sure?"

Tar didn't answer. He was too busy following the sandwich with his eyes, his expression glazed.

Daisy put the sandwich down abruptly. "You can eat it. I'm not hungry."

"The whole thing?" Tar sniffed it. "It's fresh," he muttered in a critical voice. "I suppose you can't have everything." He began to eat steadily, commenting appreciatively to himself between mouthfuls.

"I wish we still had a TV," Daisy said. It would have helped take her mind off the fact that her mum was now nearly five hours late.

"There were a lot of interesting things on TV," Daisy told Tar. "There was this one show about a huge family that lived in a tiny house. Every time they said anything at all, invisible people laughed! It was very funny."

Daisy had asked for a TV for her eleventh birthday. When the day came, however, she got a telescope instead. It was a magnificent telescope, powerful enough to see even quite distant stars. But she couldn't help feeling disappointed.

She left the kitchen and made her way upstairs to her mum's room. It comforted her a little to be surrounded by her mum's things. Her mum's long, flowery dress hanging over the chair, her glasses on the bedside table, her dozens of paintings, all turned with their faces to the wall.

Daisy lay down on the bed and hugged her mum's pillow, staring at the photograph on the bedside table. It showed her mum's family on the tennis court, years ago. It was odd to see the court free of grass and bindweed. Daisy's grandparents had just finished a game of tennis and were standing side by side with their arms around each other. Her uncle Marcus was in the picture too and behind him, a group of other people. Daisy's mum had told her all their names.

There was Mr. Hadley, who drove the car and was very kind. And the housekeeper, Maggie, with a jug of lemonade in her hand, and one of the gardeners, who had volunteered to be the umpire. And there, towards the edge of the picture, stood a tall older boy with his face half turned away.

"That's James," Daisy's mum had said when Daisy asked about him. "He was some sort of cousin. He used to visit every summer. Then he stopped coming."

"Why?"

Her mum paused. "I don't know the details," she said. "I think he stole a watch. Or they thought he had . . . I don't remember what happened."

"Where is he now?"

"I don't know," Daisy's mum said. She was never cross with

Daisy, but her voice had sounded almost sharp. "I don't know. It doesn't matter."

Now Daisy hugged her mum's pillow tighter, trying to fight the urge to look at her own watch.

Had it been five hours, or closer to six?

Perhaps she was worrying for nothing. Perhaps at that very moment, her mum was turning into the driveway. Daisy hurried downstairs. She seated herself on the stone doorstep, her gaze fixed on the distant gates. She thought perhaps if she stared for five whole minutes without blinking, it would make the car appear. Then she tried closing her eyes and counting to a thousand, not gabbling the numbers but saying each one slowly and clearly.

Nothing worked. The shadows of the great trees grew long over the tangled meadow. It was evening now. Soon it would be dark. Daisy's body flooded with panic.

She has to come back! How will she do the Day Box if she doesn't come back?

FIVE

Daisy's mum was right about the house being cluttered but not dirty. It wasn't dirty because they didn't keep any old clothes or leftover food or rubbish lying around. Instead, Brightwood Hall was filled with three kinds of things. The first was furniture and household items, most of it valuable, which had been stacked in the ballroom, the spare rooms, or against various walls. The second was stores of food and grocery items. These filled the whole of the basement, most of the reception area, and a great portion of the corridors.

The third was all the Day Boxes.

There were nearly ten thousand of them. They were about

the same size and shape as shoe boxes, except they opened from one end so that when they were stacked on top of each other, you could open one without disturbing the whole pile. At first they had all been kept in the Marble Hall. The shelving units had been specially built to hold them. But they had eventually filled up even that enormous space. They had spread into the Portrait Gallery and then into other rooms and empty corners, until you could hardly turn around without bumping into a pile of them.

Every evening, another box was added to the collection.

Daisy's mum made them. She put things inside that she wanted to remember about the day. Everything held a memory, she said. If she didn't put it into a box, the memory would fade and be lost. She would never be able to get it back again.

Daisy sometimes contributed to the Day Boxes, but mostly her mum did them on her own. After she closed the lid of each box, she wrote the date on the side. She always used the same black marker, and she would never run out of those markers because there were thirty-six packets of them down in the basement and each packet held two dozen pens.

Daisy's mum never missed a single day. Not even the time when she had a terrible fever and had lain a whole day and night moaning and shivering and saying strange things. Daisy had sat with her, cooling her face with wet towels, and in the evening, her mum had told her to fetch an empty box. Her hand crept out from under the covers to point out the things she had chosen for that day. Or maybe they were what the fever had chosen, because the things themselves didn't make much sense.

"Your shoe, Mum?" Daisy had said, putting it into the box. "Are you *sure*?"

Her mum's hand gestured feebly towards the wall.

"That's just a shadow, Mum. From the chair, see? You can't put a shadow into a box."

Now Daisy leaped up from her perch on the doorstep and hurried back into the house. She crawled across the tops of the shelves in the Marble Hall. The tight passageways below were already plunged into darkness. But the chandelier still held a faint milky glitter as it caught the last of the waning light.

She glanced into the library as she went by. The empty Day Boxes were stored there. They were made of a kind of cardboard that was almost as strong as wood. Her mum ordered them from a special shop and they were delivered twice a month.

The library was another thing that Daisy was afraid of.

There were hundreds of dark gaps in the shelves where books had been removed. Daisy knew if she slid her hand into any one of them, her fingers would meet nothing more extraordinary than the back of the bookcase. But what if they didn't? What if her fingers just kept going, and then her hand and then her whole arm? What if there was nothing back there except *nothingness*?

Daisy hurried to her bedroom and dragged a chair over to block the door. She sat on her bed with her knees pulled up tight to her chin and her arms wrapped around her legs.

How could her mum do the Day Box if she wasn't here?

Her mum was very particular about the boxes and what was put inside them. On the day she turned five, for example, Daisy had wanted to put a slice of her birthday cake into the Day Box. It had been a beautiful cake. Her mum had decorated it with real flowers and tiny animals made of frosting. But her mum had explained that you couldn't put food into the Day Box or anything that would rot and start to smell bad.

"And nothing that will die," she had said gently when Daisy once suggested including a stag beetle, which was lurching down the path.

Daisy had always been interested in beetles and other insects. There were millions and millions of them, although you mostly never saw them. They lived in a secret world. It was huge yet invisible. There were doors to this world everywhere: in the cracks of the floorboards, on the underside of leaves, although the doors were too tiny for humans. Daisy squatted next to ant nests, magnifying glass in hand, watching where the marching lines went in and out of the earth. But magnifying glasses are good at making things bigger, not smaller, and Daisy would always be too enormous to ever escape into the insect world.

She lost a lot of interest in her mum's Day Boxes after she found out that you couldn't put bugs into them. Instead her mum usually chose rather ordinary things such as books she had read, items of clothing, and other bits and bobs.

Daisy lay down on her bed still fully clothed. Slowly she pulled the blanket over her head. She rested her cheek in her hand and tried to sleep.

Mum will come back, she told herself. *Sometime in the night, I will open my eyes and there she will be.*

DAY TWO

SIX

Waking up alone the next morning was by far the worst thing that had ever happened to Daisy. She lay half paralyzed by misery, her eyes filling with tears. There was a possibility that her mum had returned and hadn't wanted to wake her up. She could be downstairs getting breakfast ready or preparing the schoolwork for the day.

But in her heart, Daisy knew this wasn't true.

She got up slowly and went into the Portrait Gallery, determined to ignore Little Charles. She wasn't in the mood for his demands.

"I found my hoop!" he cried. "Where is Minette?"

Daisy paused, despite herself. "Minette? Is she your sister?"

"Not her!" His voice was an indignant squeak. "I don't want *her*! She's just a girl and my father says girls are a waste of space. Minette is my dog . . . "

"I can't look for her now," Daisy said. "I'll look later. I promise, Little Charles."

She hurried by the General, keeping her eyes away. But she could tell he was watching her, his eyes as bright as the row of medals pinned to his scarlet chest. The house was completely silent. Fear rose in Daisy's throat. It felt the same as wanting to be sick.

She must act normal. There was nothing else to do.

It was the first Tuesday of the month. She and her mum always collected trash along the perimeter wall on that day. Daisy went to the kitchen and found a black trash bag.

The perimeter wall ran all the way around Brightwood Hall. It was fifteen feet high and made of brick. Over time, the ground beneath the wall had shifted slightly, and the bricks had left their perfectly straight lines to follow a more winding course. When they were new, they had all looked exactly the same. But sun and wind and creeping moss had left their different marks, and now each brick had its own face and its own story. Yet the wall was as strong as it had ever been.

Daisy headed around the house and down the driveway.

Beyond the perimeter wall there was a road that ran for almost the whole front of the grounds before curving away. The majority of the trash that came over the wall was in this area. Some of it came in from the wind. Mostly people threw it from the road.

"Some people just like to litter," her mum had told Daisy.

There were always a lot of plastic bags and food wrappings, although Daisy often found other, more surprising items. Sneakers with their laces tied together. A plastic thing shaped like a lollipop that her mum told her was a "pacifier" for a baby. A bottle of whiskey that was still half full. A red woolen scarf. A pair of broken eyeglasses.

Each object seemed too specific to be accidental. As if they weren't just random bits of litter, but messages of some kind, although Daisy could never quite figure out what the messages might be.

There was nothing unusual in the trash today, however. She followed the line of the wall, gathering the usual scraps. When she was finished, Daisy put the bag in the bin by the gates and walked back up the driveway.

From this distance, Brightwood Hall looked untouched by time, as elegant and grand as it had always been with its hundreds of windows glittering in the sun. You couldn't see that the flagstones were full of gaps, and the stone balcony was covered with ivy and lichen.

Daisy left the driveway and made her way across the lawn and through a clump of trees until she reached the topiary.

A long time ago, the topiary had been a magical place. It had consisted of twenty boxwood trees, all trimmed into the shapes of people and animals. There had been an elephant and a man in a top hat and a couple dancing together and a fox and a rabbit. Now all that was left were dry branches twisted around rusty metal structures. The topiary looked more like a collection of ragged skeletons than a garden. But right in the middle, one tree remained green.

It was a horse, a little smaller than life-size, with arched neck and prancing leg. Daisy stroked its leafy flank.

"Good boy, True. Good horse."

Beneath her fingers, the leaves seemed to shiver. She put her face against the horse's side to catch the strange, musky scent of the plant. It was the smell of sadness and courage. The horse didn't know how he had survived the boxwood blight that had taken his companions one by one. He didn't even know why he was a horse. Some long-ago gardener had shaped him that way to satisfy a fancy—that was all.

Yet he kept his head high. He endured.

Of all the creatures in Brightwood Hall, True was Daisy's favorite.

She reached for her waistband and pulled out a small antique hunting knife. Although it was old, it was extremely sharp and her mum had forbidden her to use it. But Daisy liked the feel of the handle and was always careful to keep the blade safe in its leather sheath. It came in useful when True needed a trim.

"I'm sorry," Daisy whispered as she cut a few ragged leaves from his nose. "It has to be done . . . "

"Yes, to keep my shape."

"To keep you True."

"It doesn't hurt very much," he admitted. True was always honest. Daisy didn't think he was capable of telling a lie.

"You're brave," she told him. She stroked his ears. "Do you know where Mum is? Do you know why she left?"

The horse was silent.

"Do you think . . . she's still angry with me? Do you think that's why she's not come home?"

Daisy and her mother hardly ever disagreed, although they'd had an argument just the week before. Daisy had wanted to go to the bulk-buy store.

"Not this time," her mum had said. She was out on the lawn with her easel, painting. She was wearing her flowery dress and her hair was tied back in a long ponytail. "One of these days, I'll take you. When you're a little older."

"I want to go *today*." Daisy wasn't sure why she felt so strongly about it. It was something to do with getting a telescope for her eleventh birthday instead of a television. The disappointment had stayed with her and turned into stubbornness.

Daisy crossed her arms and stared hard at her mother. "I want to. Why can't I?"

Her mum kept dabbing at her painting, not looking at Daisy. "All right, then," she said. "Fine. If you want to go outside so much, there's nothing stopping you." Her voice was tight.

"What, *now*?"

Her mum shrugged.

"On my *own*?"

"You said you wanted to go outside. So go."

Daisy hesitated. Her mum kept on painting, her head turned away. Daisy walked slowly down the driveway. When she got to the gates, she stopped.

Where am I meant to go? Daisy thought. *What direction should I take?*

She looked back. Her mum had stopped painting. Her shoulders were hunched. Daisy walked back up the driveway. Her mum didn't say anything, although her expression was strange. She hugged Daisy tight.

"We have everything we need right here, don't we?" her mum said. She rubbed her pale forehead and tried to smile.

"Yes," Daisy mumbled. "Yes, Mum. Of course we do."

Her mum had seemed more sad than angry. But perhaps

Daisy had been mistaken. Perhaps her mum had now left Daisy alone to punish her.

"Do you think that's the reason?" she asked True.

"No," he said immediately. "Your mum would never do that. Not in a million years."

Daisy nodded, reassured. True never lied.

"Your mum loves you," he said. "She would never leave you willingly."

Daisy stuck the knife back into her waistband. "What am I going to do?"

"You should go and get help," he said. "You should go outside."

"I *can't*!" Daisy cried. "I don't know where to go!"

True said nothing and Daisy felt ashamed.

"Maybe I *should* go," she admitted. "But I'm frightened, True. I'm not brave like you. I'm a coward—"

She turned. She had heard the distant sound of a car.

"She's back!" Daisy shouted, and dashed as fast as she could through the trees towards the driveway. But in the shadow of a bush, she stopped short.

It wasn't her mum's blue car. It was much smaller and silver in color. There was a man in the driver's seat.

SEVEN

Daisy watched as the strange car made its way up the drive, turned in a wide sweep at the top, and stopped by the entrance to the house. The car door opened and the man got out.

She brought her binoculars up to her eyes for a better look. The man was dressed in dark blue trousers and a dark blue jacket. He stepped forward a few paces with his back to Daisy, and then paused, staring up at the house. He stood so still he might have been a man pretending to be a statue.

Or a statue pretending to be a man.

Daisy's first instinct was to run. She ducked back into the trees and raced through the topiary and around the walled gardens, her legs lashed by tall thistles and meadowsweet. She ran through the kitchen door and bolted it. Then Daisy wriggled and climbed her way through the house and up the great staircase, heading for her grandfather's old study, which had the best view of the front of the grounds.

There was an earthenware vase on her grandfather's desk, which Sir Clarence the explorer had brought back from his travels. Daisy liked it because the handles were in the shape of monkeys, their arms clutching the sides of the vase. But it was almost hidden behind piles of old papers, and the rest of the room was a forest of stacked chairs and benches.

Daisy dropped to her knees and crawled a winding path through the chair legs until she reached the window. She lifted her head cautiously and peered down.

The silver car was still parked below, but there was no sign of the man. She raised herself higher. He wasn't on the driveway or the lawn.

Daisy turned and crawled back the way she had come. She was still breathing fast, but it was a different sort of breathing than before, a soft whimpering in the back of her throat.

She had just remembered that the front door was unlocked.

Daisy crept to the top of the staircase and found a hidden space behind a tall stack of books. From here, she could see the front half of the Marble Hall and the two white pillars that separated it from the reception area. Beyond the pillars, there were boxes of unopened deliveries, and the weighty oak of the front door, with its stained-glass panel at the top casting a thick, yellow light that made the bronze door handle gleam.

The door handle was moving. Daisy hunched further into her hiding place. She saw a large black shoe pressed against the edge of the door as it opened. It was the man.

He was inside the house.

He was inside the house!

Daisy wanted to crawl away to the darkest corner she could find, yet she couldn't take her eyes off the stranger. She stared at him with terrified fascination.

From this distance and angle, she could see only the top of his head and part of his face. She couldn't tell if he was young or old, but he seemed big to her, almost huge, with long, dangling arms. He walked forward a few steps and then seemed to stagger back as he entered the hall. Daisy could see the pale oval of his face turned up as he looked about.

He came forward until he was at the edge of the maze of shelving. He reached his arm into one of the passageways, turned his body sideways, and shuffled forward. It looked as if he was trying to get through. But he couldn't.

He's too big! Daisy thought with a surge of relief.

The man turned to another passageway. Again he tried to enter, and again failed. Daisy saw him shake his head.

He took something white from his pocket. A handkerchief. He wiped his hands with it and looked up, his gaze sweeping the whole hall. Daisy shrank back.

The man shook his head once more.

"Crazy," he said out loud. Daisy didn't know to whom he was talking. He didn't sound angry or sad. His voice didn't have any feeling in it at all.

"Crazy," he said again.

He backed away slowly and went out the front door.

EIGHT

Daisy had no idea what to do. Now that the first shock of seeing the man had passed, she felt far less frightened, and even a little ashamed. Perhaps her mum had told him to come. For some reason, perhaps a very simple one, although Daisy couldn't think what it was, her mum had been unable to return. Instead she had sent this man to find her and make sure she was safe.

The theory made sense. Daisy leaped to her feet and ran down the staircase and through the maze of shelving to the front door. She peered outside. The man was taking something out of his car. It was a long pole with a kind of wheel at the end of it. He reached into the car again and pulled out a clipboard.

If he had been sent to find her, what did he need a clipboard for? And why didn't he simply call her name?

The man started walking along the right side of the house, taking the path that led to the Winter Grove. As he went, he wheeled his strange contraption in front of him, pausing every now and then to write something down on his clipboard. Daisy hesitated and then began to follow.

She tracked him through the Winter Grove, a copse of trees with bright white bark, and then up around the back of the garage to the lakeside and the path with the statue of the Hunter. The man walked slowly, and although Daisy kept to the shadows, she was worried she might be seen. But he was too intent on his task to look up.

Daisy crouched down behind the Hunter.

"What's he doing?" she whispered. "Can you see?"

But the Hunter was looking in the wrong direction.

"Dark skies," he said vaguely. "Stormy waters."

Daisy saw the man disappearing behind a cluster of abandoned storage sheds. She hurried after him, keeping low. He paused to make yet another note on his clipboard and then set out towards the glasshouse in the distance.

The glasshouse was still a beautiful building even though most of the glass was broken and there were many places where there was no glass at all. Daisy thought the plants inside must have caused this damage. They had grown so big and spread so far that they had simply burst out of the place. Immediately behind the glasshouse lay the Wilderness, and Daisy thought the plants were probably responsible for that too. They had originally come from wild and jungly places, and when they escaped they encouraged all the normal, well-behaved plants outside to go wild and jungly too. Now exotic palms crowded the nettles, and orchids surprised the humble buttercups.

The Wilderness was getting bigger and bigger. It reached all the way along the north side of the property and curled around the lake on the west. There were very few paths in the Wilderness, and in many places it was difficult to get through. When the man arrived at the edge of it, he stopped short.

From the shelter of a ragged hedge that flanked the glasshouse, Daisy watched him peer into the dark undergrowth. Then, just as he had done earlier in the Marble Hall, he stepped back and shook his head.

He turned suddenly and Daisy ducked down, her heart pounding. She thought he would keep walking east, along the edge of the Wilderness, and circle around to the front through the topiary. Instead he decided to retrace his steps and headed down the path towards her. Daisy froze.

The crunch of gravel came closer. She lifted her head. He was barely five feet away. Only a thin screen of hedge separated them. All he had to do was look to the right and he would see her. But he didn't look. She watched him walk slowly by, pushing the pole with the wheel at the end of it. Up close, he was even bigger than she thought. Not fat, just tall and wide, with sloping shoulders. His hair was thin and it didn't cover the whole of his head, so his face looked longer than it was. He moved in a loose, clumsy way that made Daisy shudder slightly. As if his arms and legs weren't attached in the usual way.

As if he had been put together slightly wrong.

He veered right and entered the walled gardens. Inside, the paths were narrow, and the plants that had once grown in an orderly fashion had escaped their borders and now ran unchecked in all directions, the herbs spreading nets over the old stonework, the roses clambering in wild abandon. Daisy felt sure he would turn and see her if she followed him in there.

It suddenly occurred to her that if her mum had sent this man, she would surely have given him a key to the padlock on the front gates. All Daisy had to do was go and look.

Daisy covered the quarter mile of meadow in less than two minutes. When she got to the gates, she stopped, bent double, her chest heaving. Then she examined the huge black padlock that held the gates shut.

"Beware!" Regal said on her right.

"Be careful!" Royal whimpered to her left.

The padlock hadn't been opened with a key. It dangled from its chain, almost to the ground. The steel had been cut clean through.

Daisy stared at it in shock. Then she ran to a nearby oak tree and quickly climbed up until she reached a fork between two branches, high above. From here, she had a good view in all directions.

She wedged herself into the fork, her knees pulled tight to her chest, trying to think. She had no idea who the man was, or why he had come. The only thing she was certain of was that he had broken into Brightwood Hall. Perhaps he was a robber. What kind of robber walked around so slowly, without taking anything?

Maybe True was right. She should go. Simply climb down from the tree and leave through the gates.

But Daisy didn't know what was out there.

All she knew was what she could see, right now from this tree, with her binoculars. The distant hills, the church spire rising between the trees, and nearer the house, the stretch of road that ran for a few hundred feet before disappearing into a curve. Daisy had sat in the tree many times in the past, watching that road. Cars didn't often pass by, although when they did, she followed them with her eyes for as long as she could, marking their type and color and the outline of their passengers.

Who were those people? Where had they come from and where were they going?

Once Daisy left the grounds of Brightwood Hall, she would be completely alone. What would happen if she got lost and her mother came back in the meantime and Daisy wasn't there?

She turned her attention to the house. The man had appeared on the front lawn, still wheeling his contraption. She watched him walking to and fro for nearly an hour. As she did so, she prayed for him to vanish. She willed him to go over to his car, open the door, and drive away. This didn't happen.

Instead the man looked as if he had no intention of leaving at all.

At last he stopped walking. Daisy adjusted the focus on her binoculars. The man had put down his contraption and was standing perfectly still, staring out over the estate with his hands on his hips.

As if he owned the place.

But it was *her* place. She should get down from the tree and march right up to him and ask him what he thought he was doing. And then she should order him to leave at once.

Except she didn't. She stayed hidden in the tree, watching him.

He was on the move again, heading towards his car. He

didn't go to the driver's side. He went to the back of the car and opened the trunk, then took out a backpack and two plastic shopping bags.

He carried them around the side of the house and disappeared from view.

NINE

It was evening, but Daisy could still see the lake from her bedroom. She stood with her arms wrapped around herself, overcome by fear and worry.

The man had taken the rowboat that was tied up to a jetty not far from where the Hunter stood, and he had rowed out across the lake to the boathouse on the far side. The lake was long and narrow, and a path ran all the way around it. But the Wilderness had claimed a good deal of the path, and now the only way to get to the other side of the lake was by boat. Daisy could just see the boat from the window of her room, moored a few feet away from the boathouse door.

As she watched, a light flickered on in the boathouse. He was getting ready for the night. Making himself at home.

At least he wasn't in the main house. He couldn't enter most of the rooms, and she thought it would be almost impossible for him to get up to the second floor. But this wasn't much comfort. Perhaps he was simply waiting until morning before making another, more serious attempt to get in.

She was alone, her mum was gone, and there was nobody to help her. A wave of helplessness washed over her, as strong as any feeling she had ever known.

Daisy went to her bed and curled up into a ball, her face pressed against the pillow. If only she were as brave as the rest of her family. Like her great-great-aunt Emily Fitzjohn, who had fought as fiercely as a Roman soldier—only better, because she had to wear a long skirt—for women to get the Vote. Daisy was unclear what "the Vote" actually was, although she knew it was something important and valuable. Or Sir Clarence the explorer, who had disappeared into the Amazon jungle on his quest for the Lost City of Valcadia.

How did a person get to the Amazon? Daisy had no idea. She didn't even know how people could tell where one country ended and another began. When she was little, she used to think that your skin changed color when you went to a different country, but her mum had laughed at that.

What an imagination you have!

You can bring things to life!

If she really *could* bring things to life, she would make Sir Clarence appear. He would give himself a little shake and step right out of that old black-and-white picture, with his gun still on his shoulder.

She visualized the photograph: the background pale with heat, low trees in the distance, Sir Clarence's face in profile under his strange helmet, his boot resting on the body of the dead tiger. The tiger had been a man-eater and Sir Clarence had been forced to shoot it in self-defense. Daisy didn't know whether her mum had told her that fact or whether she had made it up. Either way, it had become the truth.

The tiger didn't look much like a man-eater. It looked more like a rug stretched on the dusty ground. Daisy pressed her hands hard against her eyes until stars bloomed behind her eyelids.

It was no good.

She couldn't bring someone to life just by thinking about them. Even if she thought so hard that her head ached.

Normally the house was full of noises, little creaks and rustles and pipes clanging and the whisper of dust settling in corners. Now it was completely silent. Daisy opened her eyes.

There was a girl leaning against the door. At least Daisy *thought* it was a girl. She looked more like a boy, with short hair and a stained white shirt. A leather bag was strapped across her body, and she had on the sort of trousers that people wore when riding horses. Daisy searched for their name.

Jodhpurs.

The jodhpurs were extremely dirty. They were covered with patches of mud, and there were several burrs and twigs snagged in the fabric.

But that wasn't the strangest thing about her. The strangest thing was that she was all in black and white.

Daisy blinked and shook her head. The girl was too solid to be a ghost. And she wasn't like Tar or Little Charles or any of the other people that Daisy spoke to. They lived in the gap between real and not real. This girl looked as if she had stepped right over that gap. Daisy knew she didn't exist, although the girl didn't seem to care what Daisy thought. She was right there in her bedroom, and by the look on her face, she didn't seem terribly impressed by what she saw.

Daisy wondered whether she was a hallucination. She closed her eyes and counted to three, but when she opened them again, the girl was still there, as solid as ever.

Daisy had once read a story about a little boy who had a dog that only he could see. She searched her mind for the phrase.

"Are you . . . are you an imaginary friend?" Daisy ventured.

The girl didn't answer. She had a knife stuck into her belt on one side. A metal container hung on the other. Daisy thought it might be for water.

"So *this* is the Lost City of Valcadia," the girl said in a brisk voice. She looked around, her eyes bright in her dirty face. "Not exactly what I was expecting."

"It's not the Lost City," Daisy protested. "It's not lost at all. I live here!"

"Of course it's not *really* lost," the girl said with a touch of impatience. "These places never are. Not to the people living in them at any rate."

The girl paused. "Can I be perfectly honest?"

Daisy nodded, although she had the feeling that the girl wasn't really asking a question and would have gone on talking whether Daisy agreed or not.

"The only thing in the world that's *really* lost," the girl continued, "is Sir Clarence himself!"

She stepped forward. "He'll be pleased if he ever does get here," she commented. "There are enough artifacts in this place to keep him going for ages."

"Artifacts?"

The girl swung her arm over the cluttered room.

"Artifacts! Sir Clarence is very fond of them."

Daisy was about to ask her again what she meant, but she stopped herself. It was absurd how quickly she had accepted this

71

strange girl's presence. Even the fact that she was in black and white didn't seem odd any longer. A long time ago, Daisy had seen a television show that had been in black and white, and had gotten used to it after a moment or two. This was exactly the same.

"You're not in the photograph with Sir Clarence," Daisy said, trying to assert herself. "I don't even know who you are!"

The girl gave her a scornful look.

"Of course I'm not in the picture! I was the one who took it."

"Oh," Daisy said, feeling crushed.

"You can't be in two places at *exactly* the same time," the girl said as if she was explaining something to a child.

You can't appear out of thin air or be in black and white either, Daisy thought. For somebody who wasn't real, the girl had no right to be so bossy. But she didn't want to point this out. She didn't want the girl to disappear and leave her on her own again.

At the same time, she couldn't help feeling disappointed.

"I thought . . . "

"You thought you'd get *him*? Sir Clarence?" The girl tossed her dark head. "You're better off with me. By far."

"Who are you?"

"Polly Frank. You can forget the Polly bit. I'm just Frank. Sir Clarence's chief guide, chief tracker, and chief navigator. In charge of provisions, maps, and all staff."

"All staff?"

"Well, there's just the two of us," Frank admitted. "But I do the work of ten. If it weren't for me, Sir Clarence would be dead a hundred times over. I've saved him from everything. Quicksand, cannibals, worms in the gut, alligators, landslides, animal traps, flash floods, human sacrifice, and heatstroke. The man is an idiot. Brave of course, although still an idiot."

"I don't think that can be true," Daisy protested. "He was a famous explorer. He almost became the first man to get to the top of Mount Everest!"

"Oh certainly!" Frank cried, "if by 'almost' you mean crippled by diarrhea down at base camp while I was busy on the summit."

"You mean . . . *you* were the first person to get to the top?"

"It's a little-known fact," Frank said, brushing the front of her grubby shirt with an air of unconcern. "I'm not one to boast . . . " She strode over to the window and stood looking out over the darkening water. "So what have we got here?" she demanded. "An intruder, I take it?"

Daisy nodded.

"What's his name?"

"I don't know."

"He must have come upriver," Frank commented. "I took the jungle route myself."

"It's not a river, it's a lake," Daisy said. "And he came in a car."

"Particularly hazardous, that stretch of jungle," Frank continued, as if Daisy hadn't spoken. "You can hack through the undergrowth all day and still only travel a hundred feet. Easy to start walking in circles. I believe that's what's happened to Sir Clarence."

"It's not a jungle!" Daisy cried. "It's just the meadow and trees and stuff—"

"What is he doing here?" Frank interrupted.

"I don't know."

"You don't know much, do you?"

Frank swung her leather bag to the front of her body, reached inside, and pulled out a pair of ancient binoculars.

"What else have you got in that bag?" Daisy asked.

"I've got everything in here," Frank said with satisfaction.

"Everything? For what?"

"For survival."

DAY THREE

TEN

The first thing Daisy thought when she woke up the next morning was how much she would have liked to see inside Frank's bag. She hadn't gotten the chance, because the minute she took her eyes off her, the girl had vanished. Perhaps Frank was bored with talking to Daisy—or she had heard Sir Clarence calling.

Or perhaps she had been nothing but a dream.

Daisy got out of bed and went to the window to look for the rowboat. The sky was overcast and a low mist hung over the lake. But she could see that the boat was moored on the far side, which meant the man must still be at the boathouse.

Daisy hurried downstairs for breakfast, suddenly ravenous. She had eaten hardly anything the day before. Little Charles's voice was a thin pipe as she went by.

"More space!"

"I can't. I have to find out what the man is up to."

"Set the dogs on him," Little Charles advised. "My father set the dogs on a poacher once. They tore him to pieces!"

"That's terrible," Daisy said.

"It was all right," Little Charles said. "He was only a commoner, you know."

"You're not being very helpful," Daisy told him.

Tar wasn't very helpful either. He scurried up onto the kitchen counter as soon as Daisy had cut herself a thick slice of bread.

"Smells good," he remarked, his nose twitching, ignoring her attempts to bat him away. "There are five kinds of smell in the world. First comes *rich* and then comes *ripe*. Perfectly good smells, but *rank* is better. After *rank* comes *rancid*. I'm very partial to *rancid* . . . "

"I can't be thinking about smells now," Daisy protested. "I have to eat and then I have to go out and . . . confront that man. I'm scared, Tar. I'm really scared."

Tar made a dive for the crust of bread on Daisy's plate. "Last stage is *rotten*," he announced with his mouth full. "Nothing better than a good rotten smell. Brings tears to my eyes."

"Do you want to come with me?"

But Tar was gone. He was only a friend when there was food to be had. It wasn't his fault. It was just the way rats were.

She unbolted the kitchen door, slipped outside, and made her way to the front of the house to have a look at the man's car. But there was nothing to be learned from it. It was perfectly ordinary looking, apart from a long scrape down the left-hand side.

The mist was still thick over the lake. Daisy could barely see the surface of the water, and the Wilderness beyond it was just a green haze. She waited at the base of the Hunter's statue.

"Are you frightened?" she asked him.

"Mine heart is all courage," the Hunter muttered in a terrified voice.

"Don't worry," she told him, feeling a little braver by comparison.

There was a movement out on the lake. The mist had formed a clump that seemed to writhe and swirl. Then the boat emerged with the man at the oars. He was far too big for the vessel and he handled it clumsily, with scooping, uneven movements that sent the boat lurching along. Despite this, he made surprisingly quick progress across the lake, and in a few moments, he was drawing close to the little jetty, barely twenty feet from where Daisy stood. He lunged forward, looping the boat's rope around the post at the end of the jetty, and then hauled himself out onto dry land.

Daisy stepped out from behind the Hunter so suddenly that the man staggered back with surprise.

"What are you doing here?" he said, advancing towards her. "This is private property."

Now that the moment had come to say something, Daisy couldn't summon a single word. Apart from her mum, she had never been near a real, living person in her whole life. The man was so close she could see into his eyes. They were light blue and she couldn't stop staring at them. It wasn't their color; it was that there was so *much* color. The black bits in the middle—the pupils—were barely any larger than pinholes.

They reminded Daisy of something, although she didn't know what it was.

"How did you get in?" the man demanded.

Daisy had no good answer for this. She had gotten in by being born. But that seemed so obvious that it felt stupid to point out. She had taken all night to come into the world, and there had been nobody in the house to help her mum. When she'd finally arrived, her mum had cried. Not because she was sad, but because she was so happy. It was the happiest moment of her whole life, she said.

"Are you deaf?" the man said. "What's your name?"

"Daisy," she whispered.

"What did you say?"

"Daisy. Daisy Fitzjohn."

He stared at her. "That's not true," he said. "There's no such person."

"There is," Daisy said. "It's me."

"I don't believe you."

Daisy felt tears pricking at her eyes. She didn't understand why he was questioning her. "It *is* me," she insisted. "I live here. There's a picture of me in the hallway. My mum painted it."

The man said nothing. His pale eyes were expressionless and his big hands hung loosely by his side.

"How old are you?" he said at last in a low voice.

"Eleven."

"Eleven? It's not possible." He paused. "Unless . . . "

"Who else lives here?" he asked. "Who looks after you?"

Daisy didn't know why he seemed so agitated.

"It's just us," she said. "Just me and my mum." There was no stopping her tears now. "Do you know where she is?" she cried out. "Do you know why she hasn't come back?"

He was silent, watching her.

"No," he said at last. "I don't know where she is."

"Then . . . why did you come?"

"I was just passing by," the man said. "I didn't know you were here."

"You broke the lock on the gates!" Daisy protested.

He didn't seem to have heard her. He gazed at her thoughtfully. The sun came out, evaporating the mist on the lake, and the man's face darkened in the sudden shadow of the Hunter.

"Where do you go to school?" he asked.

"In the ballroom," Daisy said.

"The ballroom?"

"My mum teaches me. We're learning about the Romans . . . "

"But you do go out? To the doctor for checkups or to play with friends?"

Daisy was silent.

"Perhaps your mother takes you out for trips," he said.

"My mum says she's going to take me when . . . when I'm older."

He stepped forward out of the shadow and she saw his eyes again, the blue very pale in the bright light.

"You mean you've *never* been out? Not even once? You must have tried, sneaked out by yourself from time to time?"

Daisy lowered her head. He made it sound as if it was strange that she hadn't gone out, as if she'd done something wrong by not trying. But she had only been doing what she'd been told.

"I'm not allowed," she whispered, feeling her cheeks grow hot.

"How about visitors, then?" the man said.

The tears rose in Daisy's eyes once again. How many questions was he going to ask her? Why wouldn't he stop? She was the one who was meant to be finding out about *him*. He had turned it the other way around.

"Surely you have visitors," he continued. "Other children perhaps? Friends of your mother?"

She shook her head desperately, helplessly.

"Plumbers?" the man persisted. "Repairmen . . . "

"We don't need that," Daisy said. "When something breaks, we get a new one."

"Are you saying you've never been outside and you've never . . . you've never even had a visitor?"

For a split second, she saw his eyes flood black. Then his pupils shrank back again.

"Nobody knows you're here," he said in a wondering voice. "Nobody knows you exist."

ELEVEN

Daisy felt herself start to tremble inside.

"I just want to find my mum!" she cried. "I have to go and find her!"

"I don't think that's a good idea," the man said quickly. He paused and then smiled, as if it was an afterthought. "We should both wait here until your mother gets back. I think that would be the most sensible thing to do. What do you say?"

Daisy opened her mouth to say she didn't care what he thought and she didn't want to wait anywhere with him. In fact, she wanted him to leave right that minute. But the trembling had reached her throat and she couldn't utter a single word.

Instead, Daisy turned and ran away.

"Hey! Come back!" he shouted. He ran after her and she ran even faster: Around the back towards the glasshouse and then left, straight into the Wilderness, through nettles and bramble bushes, barely feeling the stings and scratches.

The trees grew thick and Daisy slowed down, stumbling over roots, branches whipping at her arms and face. At last she stopped and stood with her back to the trunk of a tree, as if she had reached the very end of the world and could go no farther.

Her face was wet. She was crying. She could hear her own quiet sobbing and the sound of the wind in the topmost branches.

Nobody knows you're here. Nobody knows you exist.

The moment the man had said it, she had known it was true. And she realized that she had always known. She had known without speaking about it, or even thinking about it. It was so obvious, how could she *not* have known? Her life wasn't normal. It was peculiar, perhaps even wrong.

Her face burned with shame. Far off she heard the sound of clanking metal. It came from Brightwood Hall's old stable yard, abandoned for a hundred years in the deepest part of the Wilderness. Daisy hated the stables, with their double doors hanging agape and their ancient darkness. The clanking came from a huge, rusty chain that dangled from a post and swayed in the wind, turning and twitching like something that should not be alive but was.

She crouched down and pressed her hands tight against her ears.

All this time, she had thought of the outside world as a strange place, hard to imagine. But it wasn't. It was the other way around.

It was Daisy herself who was strange and hard to imagine.

"Can I be perfectly honest?" Daisy looked up. The girl, Frank, was standing on the far side of the clearing. She still appeared in black and white, and the contrast was even clearer in the dappled sunlight, as if her outline had been sharpened by a knife.

"You don't want to be sitting on the ground like that for any length of time," Frank said. "Not in terrain like this."

"Why not?"

"Where do I begin? You've got your army ants, your vipers, and your venomous spiders, just for a start. Then there are the leeches. You ever heard of the saber-toothed leech?"

Daisy shook her head.

"Not many have," Frank said. "It's more of a biter than a sucker. It burrows. Looks for points of entry." She paused and made a face. "Your ears, your nose, your mouth, your b—"

"That's disgusting!" Daisy scrambled to her feet.

Frank patted her survival bag. "I've got most of the antivenoms in here, but if you're bitten by a saber-toothed leech, you're on your own."

"Even Sir Clarence knows *that*," she added.

Daisy decided it was time to put her foot down. "I don't live in a lost city and this isn't a jungle," she said firmly. "There aren't any army ants or leeches lurking around."

"Army ants don't lurk," Frank said. "They march. Sometimes in a straight line, sometimes in a fan formation." She slapped an invisible insect on her arm and then flicked it off with a matter-of-fact gesture. "Why are you sitting around blubbing, anyway?" she asked.

Daisy's shoulders drooped. "Nobody knows I exist," she said.

Frank let out her breath in a long, exasperated sigh. "Like I said, I've got a lot of things in my survival bag. I've got a penknife with fifty-nine blades, water purifying equipment, first aid kit, compass—not that I need it, because I can make my own out of a plain old pin and a plain old leaf anytime I want—matches, flint, peppermints, collapsible hat, collapsible cooking pan, collapsible stove."

Daisy stared at the bag doubtfully. It didn't look big enough to hold quite that many items.

"Breathing tube for avalanches," Frank continued. "Two-man tent, a bottle for messages when you're cast away on a desert island, fishing hooks, splinter extractor, night vision goggles, and a spare pair of socks."

Frank stopped for breath. "Among *many* other things," she added. "But I don't have anything for your problem." She folded her arms across her chest and stared hard at Daisy. "There's a simple reason for that."

"What?" Daisy asked.

"Because it's stupid," Frank said.

Daisy was so outraged that for a second or two, she couldn't speak.

"That's easy for you to say!" she burst out.

"We're wasting time," Frank said. "This man. Who is he and what's he doing here?"

"I don't know," Daisy admitted.

"You didn't even *ask*?"

"I wanted to," Daisy began. "But it was hard. He kept—"

"Never mind," Frank said with an impatient gesture. "I need to think."

She began to pace back and forth across the clearing with a look of deep concentration. There wasn't much space for walking, and when she got to a bush or a rock, Daisy expected she would simply pass through it, in the manner of a ghost. But she didn't. Instead the obstacle itself appeared to move, shifting out of her path in a way that made Daisy blink and rub her eyes.

"I've got it," Frank said at last, still striding to and fro.

"What?"

"The padlock was cut, wasn't it? That means the man must have arrived with a pair of metal cutters. And the wheel thing he keeps pushing around. He brought that too."

"I don't understand."

"He has *equipment*," Frank said. "That can only mean one thing."

"What?"

"He's a rival explorer," Frank announced. "Got to be."

Daisy couldn't help feeling disappointed. The explanation was completely ridiculous.

"I really don't think—" she began.

"There's always a race to be the first in a new place," Frank interrupted. "I've seen it before. Not with Sir Clarence, of course. No chance of him ever being the first to find anything. He can't find his own boots without a map, and even then it's touch and go. No, it's obvious. This man wants the Lost City all for himself. All the artifacts, everything."

Daisy thought of the bags the man had taken from the trunk of his car.

"Those are his supplies," Frank told her. "His provisions. He's set up camp." She shook her head. "It doesn't look good. Things could get ugly."

She glanced at the knife sticking out of Daisy's waistband, which Daisy had used to prune True.

"You might want to brush up on your knife-throwing skills."

"I don't have any knife-throwing skills," Daisy said, pulling the blade out.

"Never too late to start," Frank said.

Daisy squared her shoulders and squinted uncertainly at a nearby tree stump.

"Nothing to it," Frank said.

Daisy threw the knife at the stump. It bounced off with a thud.

"It's a knife," Frank said in a condescending voice. "Not a paintbrush!"

Daisy gritted her teeth but kept silent. She threw the knife again. It missed the stump, although at least it flew blade-first this time, landing with a satisfying stab into the ground.

"Stop flinging your arm," Frank commanded. "You want a short, chopping action." She sighed and shook her head. "First, Sir Clarence and now you. Why do I always get stuck with such amateurs?"

TWELVE

The man was waiting for her at the edge of the Wilderness. While she had been gone, the day had grown hot, and the sky was blue and empty. The man had taken off his jacket. There were wet stains under the arms of his shirt.

"There you are," he said, with the same pause between his words and smile as before. He had a plastic bag in his hand. It was filled with the tiny strawberries that grew wild all through the walled gardens. "I got them for you," he said. "A peace offering."

Daisy hesitated, not moving any closer.

"Who are you?" she said.

His face went still as if he was thinking. "I used to come here," he said at last. "A long time ago."

He hadn't answered the question. Daisy wanted to repeat it in a louder voice, but the man was talking again, his words coming fast.

"I upset you. It was the surprise of seeing you here. Why don't we start all over again?" He held out the bag of strawberries. "We could have tea. Do you know how to make tea?"

Daisy nodded. "I can cook a lot of things."

"Of course you can," the man said. "Of course you can."

His voice was kind, and he was careful to keep his distance as they made their way back to the house, not even coming into the kitchen but waiting outside while Daisy boiled water in the kettle. She began to think he wasn't as bad as Frank had said.

Perhaps he wasn't bad at all. Daisy risked a quick glance out the window. The man looked nothing like a rival explorer. Frank was completely wrong about that.

Tar came running up as soon as he heard the kettle whistle. Daisy hustled him into her pocket before he could protest. There were a few leftover crumbs at the bottom that would keep him busy for a while.

She made the tea and put the cups on a tray, together with a bowl for the strawberries, then carried it out carefully. The man was sitting at the little table where she and her mum sometimes had breakfast when the weather was nice. Daisy put the tray down and, after hesitating for a second or two, sat opposite him.

"How nice," the man said. "I'll pour, shall I?"

Daisy nodded. She had to hold the cup in both hands to stop herself from trembling and spilling the tea. She took a sip without tasting it, the liquid burning her tongue. The man carefully transferred the strawberries from the plastic bag into the bowl and pushed it to the center of the table.

"Please, he said, "help yourself."

Daisy didn't feel able to eat anything at all. But she managed to smile politely.

"I'm sorry if I seemed rude before," the man said, taking a sip of his tea, his pale eyes fixed on Daisy's face. "Part of it was the shock of seeing Brightwood Hall in this state. It used to be so different, you see."

Daisy stared at him blankly.

"All the stuff piled up," the man explained. "All those boxes . . . in the Marble Hall. What are they?"

"They're just my mum's Day Boxes," Daisy said.

"The grounds have become so overgrown," the man continued, as if he hadn't heard. "They used to be really impressive, you know. Now there are more weeds than anything else. And the woods must be full of vermin."

Daisy didn't know what "vermin" was, although it sounded horrible.

"Oh no," she said quickly. "It's just rabbits and rats and hedgehogs and a fox."

"You can't have vermin running all over the place," the man said as if she hadn't spoken. "You need to do something about that."

Tar wriggled in Daisy's pocket and then darted out onto the table in search of things to eat. The man flinched when he saw him.

"What's that? Is that your pet?"

Tar wasn't a pet. He was just himself. "He's a friend," Daisy said.

Tar ran across the table and stopped in front of the man, wrinkling his nose. Then he ran back to Daisy. She caught him and put him back in her pocket, pinching the top of it to keep it closed.

"A friend," the man said, shaking his head. "I suppose you have a lot of 'friends' like this. Poor girl. It must be lonely here all by yourself."

Daisy had never thought she was lonely. But the way he said it made it seem true.

The man breathed out a long sigh and leaned back in his chair. She could hear the creak of the delicate wood as he rested his full weight against it.

"Your mother," he said, shaking his head again. "She needed help."

"I *do* help!" Daisy cried. "I help mow the lawn and cook supper and collect trash and . . . a lot of things!"

"I don't mean *that* kind of help," the man said. His gaze flickered away, roaming over the house behind Daisy.

"Crazy . . . " he said, as if to himself.

It was the same word he'd used in the Marble Hall when he'd first arrived. Daisy didn't understand what he meant by it. The Crazy had skipped them. Her mum had told her so. The General had The Crazy, not her mum.

The General had been her mum's great-great-uncle, and he had caused a thousand men to die somewhere in Africa. The men had been fighting all day and had run out of ammunition. When evening came, the General ordered them to fix bayonets to their empty guns and charge directly into the cannon of the enemy. He sat on his horse and watched them all die. One man had tried to run in the other direction, and the General had taken out his own gun and shot him for being a deserter and a coward.

Everyone knew the General was insane to do this, although it would have caused a great scandal to admit it. Instead they gave him another medal. The king himself presented it to him, and it lay right there on the General's chest in the Portrait Gallery.

Great-great-great-cousin Gracie had The Crazy too. She liked to catch small animals and hurt them and had to be kept locked up in her room. Luckily she had died of the flu when she was only eighteen years old. The Crazy ran through the Fitzjohn family like the boxwood blight. But it hadn't appeared for a great while.

It had been gone for so long, it might never come back, her mum said.

"Mum hasn't got The Crazy," Daisy told the man. "She's a good person!"

He made a face. Daisy couldn't tell if he was smiling or frowning.

"Let's talk about something else," he said. "How about you have a strawberry?" He pushed the bowl nearer to her with the tips of his fingers. "The little ones are the sweetest."

He was right. The little strawberries tasted the best, and it was just the right time of year for them. Daisy, however, had no appetite.

"I'll eat them later," she said.

"Promise?"

She nodded.

He stared at her in silence for a moment and then pushed back his chair.

"Well," he said, "I noticed some tools in the gardening shed. I might as well get started on those weeds."

Daisy wanted to tell him to leave the weeds alone. They weren't *his* weeds. And this wasn't his house, although he was acting as if he lived here. But he looked so big when he stood up, big enough to blot out the sun, and Daisy was afraid.

He's only trying to be nice, she told herself.

She took the bowl of strawberries and went inside, making sure to lock the kitchen door.

THIRTEEN

Daisy watched the man from the window of her grandfather's old study for nearly an hour. He spent the whole time in the front part of the grounds, slicing at the meadowsweet and nettles with a pair of shears. If Frank had been there to comment, she might have said he was hacking his way through deepest jungle, although Daisy thought the man's behavior was more random than that. His attack on the vegetation didn't seem to have any method. He simply moved from one place to another, choosing plants as if by whim. And she couldn't help feeling that he took a kind of glee in the deadly snip of the shears, beheading the tall thistles with a flourish of his arms, demolishing the trail-ing honeysuckle at a single stroke.

Daisy turned away from the window, her hands clenched.

When she looked again, the man was gone. Daisy went up to her bedroom and saw him rowing back across the lake to the boathouse. She waited until she felt fairly sure he wasn't coming back, then made her way outside to the topiary.

She sat in the middle, with her back against True.

"He wasn't weeding at all," she told the horse. "He was just cutting."

Daisy looked at the skeletal forms of the long-dead bushes. The creeping stems of a morning glory plant had wound their way up one of the legs of the smallest elephant and produced a single flower, a blue star with faded, curling petals. The flower was right in the place where the elephant's eye used to be, and for a moment, Daisy thought the animal was looking at her.

"If nobody knows you exist, how do *you* know you exist?" she asked True.

She felt his leaves brushing her cheek.

"How do you know if you're real?" she said.

"You feel the wind," he suggested. "You see the clouds pass-ing overhead. You hear the hum of the earth turning."

"But how can you be sure?" Daisy said. "How can you be

sure you're not imagining it? Or somebody else is. What if someone is just imagining me? Like a character in a book. Do characters in books know they're only made-up?"

She felt the start of tears.

"Close your eyes," True told her. "Are they closed?"

Daisy nodded.

"Be still. Listen. Deep inside you, deeper than your mind and deeper than your heart, something lies hidden. Nothing can touch it, not the gardener's shears, not rain or storm, not even the boxwood blight. Can you feel it?"

Daisy felt the slow surge of her breath and the beating of her heart.

"I . . . don't know."

"Concentrate," True said.

She opened her eyes and stared up at the calm, endless sky until something unfurled within her that was just as calm and just as endless.

"That's your Shape," True told her. "That's how you know you exist. And you have to keep your Shape, Daisy. No matter what happens."

"I will," she said. "I promise I will."

She sat for a while in silence, with the sun on her face. Then she took out her knife to practice her throwing. Frank was right. It was far better to use a chopping action. Her knife still mostly landed far from her target, but sometimes it hit and then the knife bit deep into the wood and stayed there, the handle quivering from the force of the impact.

After a short time, Daisy felt better. She stood up and brushed herself off and started back towards the house. It was getting late. She would make something to eat. Some soup perhaps and the strawberries that the man had picked for her. She trotted down the path that led to the kitchen door.

But well before she got there, her worry came back. She had just remembered something odd that the man had said over tea. He had been talking about her mum.

She needed help, he had said.

Her mum was missing. The man had said he didn't know where she was or what had happened to her.

So why had he spoken about her in the past tense?

FOURTEEN

I thought I was hungry, but I'm not," Daisy told Tar. "I'm too worried about Mum to be hungry."

"There's no such thing as not hungry," Tar commented, eyeing the bowl of strawberries on the table. "There's only *peckish, starving, ravenous,* and *ready-to-eat-your-own-leg.* I've eaten three breakfasts and four lunches today, and I'm still at the starving level."

Daisy turned and opened the fridge. There was an unopened carton of cream at the back. It would go nicely with the strawberries and might tempt her appetite. She heard the sound of claws skittering across wood.

"Tar?"

She whirled around. The rat's nose was buried in the strawberries.

"I was just going to eat those!" Daisy cried. She picked up the bowl. "Did you lick them?"

Tar didn't say anything, although he had a guilty look. .

"I can't take the chance," Daisy said. "What a waste." She took the strawberries and emptied them into the bin. "I don't want to be mean, Tar, but humans can get sick from rats."

She rinsed the bowl in the sink and put it on the side to dry.

"Tar?"

He was on the floor, moving slowly, his head held low.

"What's the matter?"

Tar shivered and stopped moving. His front paws jerked. Daisy fell to her knees beside him.

"Are you okay?"

He opened his mouth to say something, yet no sound came out. He gave her a piteous look. She scooped him up with both hands and spun around, looking for a place to put him. Then she took off her cardigan and made a nest with it in the corner of the kitchen. She placed him gently in its folds.

"Is that better?"

He didn't move. His eyes were closed. Daisy stroked his fur.

"You had too many meals today. You've eaten yourself sick."

She lowered her head and listened to his breathing. It sounded raspy.

"Are you thirsty?"

Daisy left the kitchen and clambered through the house to the Portrait Gallery, heading for an area piled high with Day Boxes from a few months before. There was a tiny baby's bottle in one of them. It had belonged to a doll. Daisy hadn't played with the doll for a long while, but the bottle had turned up in the bottom of a drawer while she was tidying her room, and her mum had included it in the box for that day.

She searched among the boxes, opening flaps and peering inside. After a moment or two, she found the one with the bottle. It was just the right size. She scrambled back to the kitchen and filled it with water.

"Tar?" She knelt down beside him. His eyes were still closed.

Daisy put the tip of the baby bottle into his mouth, squeezing it gently. But he didn't swallow. "Please," she begged. "Please try."

She could feel him trembling as she stroked him.

"It's all right," she said. "It's going to be all right."

The shadows grew long over the kitchen floor. Daisy tried again to give him water.

"Please, please, don't die," she said. "I'll tell you a story. It starts off sad, although you mustn't worry, because it has a happy ending. Are you listening, Tar?"

Beneath her fingers, his heart beat slow.

"My mum tells me this story. It's the story of her. When she was little, this house was full. There was her family, her mum and dad and brother, and there were lots of people who helped with everything. Her dad was tall and he smelled of lemons, and her mum was the most beautiful woman in the world and she smelled of flowers and new clothes."

Daisy stroked Tar's head. "I'm telling you what they smelled like because I know you're interested in smells. But the next bit of the story is sad. They had a boat—a really big one. One day they all went out for a lovely trip, but my mum lost something. Or rather, her doll lost something. It's easy to get muddled up because the doll had the same name as my mum, and she also looked exactly like her. Anyway, Mum got off the boat and it sailed without her and there was a terrible accident and she never saw any of her family ever again.

"She wasn't completely alone, of course," Daisy continued. "She still had her granny and the people who looked after the house. So she was okay. But she wasn't happy. She didn't want to go to school anymore or ever leave the house. They got tutors for her so she could learn at home. Then, when she was around fifteen, her granny died. And lots of the old servants left.

"My mum was good at painting, and when she got a bit older, she tried going away to a place called a college so she could learn how to do it better. But she was lonely. She missed home every single minute of every single day. When she met my dad, she thought he might stop her from feeling so lonely, but he couldn't. So she came back here to be on her own.

"Then I arrived," Daisy said. "And that made everything better. My mum says we don't need anyone else. Because we have our home and we have each other forever."

She glanced down at Tar.

"That's the good bit of the story," she told him. "I told you there was a happy ending." Her voice trembled. She leaned forward with the baby bottle.

The water trickled out of Tar's mouth and wet his paws.

He was gone. He was never coming back.

"Hey," Tar said in a feeble voice as he opened his eyes. "Am I dead?"

"No," Daisy cried. "You're alive!" She wanted to kiss him although she knew he would hate it.

"I *ought* to be dead," Tar said. "I ought to have gone to the great sewer in the sky. But rats have ten lives."

"I didn't know that."

"Cats only have *nine*," Tar said with great scorn. His voice was growing stronger by the second. He sniffed the baby bottle of water. "I can't drink this, it's terrible. Water should be nice and dark and swimmy."

"Swimmy?"

"With bits in it," he explained. "Swamp water is nice and swimmy. Puddle water's sometimes good too." He sniffed the bottle again. "This is from a *tap*!" he exclaimed. "It's brand-new! Got no vintage at all!"

"I did my best," Daisy said. "It was your fault you got sick. You shouldn't eat so much."

"What nonsense!" Tar said. He wiped his whiskers and gave his hindquarters a good scratch.

"This a raisin?" he asked, nibbling at her cardigan.

"No, it's a button."

"Can you eat it?"

"No."

"What's the point of it, then?"

"I love you, Tar," Daisy said. But he had run away.

Daisy tidied up the kitchen and wiped down the surfaces. Then she went back up to the Portrait Gallery to put the baby bottle back.

Her mum was strict about keeping things in the right Day Box.

Before she closed the lid, she looked to see what else was in there. She reached in and pulled everything out of the box. There was a rolled-up piece of paper, a scarf, and an envelope.

The scarf was bright blue. Daisy remembered her mum wearing it. That was after the only real snowstorm of the winter.

It had snowed all night, and in the morning, Daisy and her mum had gone out to play. Brightwood Hall was perfectly white, glittering like sugar in the wintry light. The only color to be seen was the blue of her mum's scarf and the hint of pink in her pale cheeks as she and Daisy made a huge snow rabbit out on the lawn.

Daisy couldn't help thinking that it was a terrible waste to put the scarf into the Day Box. It was so soft and beautiful.

She unrolled the piece of paper. It was a list of things from the bulk-buy store. It was all printed out, and Daisy guessed the store had given it to her mum to remind her of everything she had bought and to tell her how much it had all cost. It was a long list. Daisy couldn't get to the end of it because the paper kept trying to roll up again as fast as she unrolled it.

The day before, the man had pointed out something very obvious to Daisy, and now something different although equally obvious occurred to her.

Even if they lived for two hundred years, they would never get through the boxes of cereal, the sacks of flour, the bags of pasta, and all the other food down in the basement and stacked in the reception area. Even if they stopped using electricity, they would never use up the horde of candles, the flashlight batteries, or the LED lights. And even if they wrapped the house itself in string, there would still be hundreds of balls left over.

Why did her mum buy so much stuff? The question made

Daisy feel sad and frightened at the same time. Yet her mum always looked so happy when she came home from her shopping, humming as she sorted through the provisions and made a note in the log for each new item. And every week, the walls of groceries grew a little higher.

"I know it's a lot," her mum had told Daisy, "but you never know what you might need. Better to be safe than sorry."

Crazy, the man had called her. *She needed help.*

He was wrong. It wasn't true. Then Daisy wondered how she could be so sure. She had never known anything different, after all.

She forced the thought away and turned her attention to the last item in the box, the envelope.

There was handwriting on the outside. Her mum's name and their address here at Brightwood Hall. The writing was neat and easy enough to read, but the dots above the *i*'s and *j*'s were odd. They were very large, as if someone had gone over them several times with the pen, pressing down on the paper with almost enough force to tear it.

There was something heavy in the envelope. Daisy tipped it into her hand.

It was a watch. Daisy had never seen it before. It was made of gold, the sort of watch a man might wear, she guessed. On the back there were words engraved in flowing letters:

For my darling Tony
I will love you for all time.
Anne

Daisy ran a finger over the words, reading them again and again. Tony and Anne were the names of her mum's parents. They had gone out on their yacht and never come back. She flipped the watch over.

On the front it said *Rolex,* and around the dial there were tiny diamonds. It was a beautiful watch. Or it had been beautiful once. Now the glass was shattered and the hands hung crooked, and even though Daisy shook it and held it to her ear, she couldn't hear a tick.

It didn't look as if it had been dropped or accidentally bumped.

It looked as if someone had taken a hammer and hit it once, very hard and sharp, exactly where it would cause the most damage.

DAY FOUR

FIFTEEN

Little Charles called out to Daisy on her way downstairs the next morning. His voice was anguished.

"You have to find my dog! My Minette!"

Daisy stood on her tiptoes and peered through the gap in the books.

"She needs to poop!" Little Charles said. "It's urgent!"

Daisy frowned. If she widened the gap between the two piles of books, the piles themselves might collapse. But she'd promised Little Charles that she would find him more room. She held her breath as she carefully pushed a few more books aside. The piles wobbled slightly yet held.

Minette's body appeared. She was gray, with a long, thin snout and shaggy body. Little Charles gave a whoop.

"I didn't think you needed to poop if you were painted," Daisy said.

"You don't," Little Charles said. "It was a trick."

"You'd better be careful," Daisy said, "or I'll cover you up again."

"You'd do that?"

Daisy sighed. "No," she admitted. "I'd never do that to you, Little Charles."

It had been a couple of days since Daisy had fed the animals. She fetched the birdseed, went out the front door, and veered right, heading towards the Winter Grove on the far western side of the estate.

It was more of an avenue than a grove, a broad, sandy path with Himalayan birch trees on either side. Their trunks were pure white, and in winter they made a dazzling display against the cold sky. Now they were hung with a canopy of silvery leaves that sent lace shadows dancing across the path.

Daisy walked slowly, scattering seed to her left and right. There were a lot of thrushes in this area, and it was a favorite haunt of squirrels. Today, however, it was quiet. Then, so abruptly it made her start, a crow shrieked from the far trees. Daisy looked up.

The man was standing at the end of the path with a black trash bag in his hand. He hadn't seen her. He was looking in the other direction.

Daisy froze in sudden recognition. The way he held himself, with his face half turned away, she had seen it before. He was posed in exactly the same way in the photograph on her mum's bedside table. He was far younger then, no more than a boy, but now that she had spotted the resemblance, Daisy wondered how she could have missed it up till then.

That's James. He was some sort of cousin.

He had told her he used to visit Brightwood Hall a long time ago. Daisy felt a surge of reassurance. He had been a guest here, a member of the family.

Just then the man looked up and saw her, and Daisy risked a tiny smile.

"Didn't you enjoy the strawberries?" he said, walking towards her.

Daisy felt her face grow hot. She didn't want to tell him that she had been forced to throw his gift away.

"Well, never mind," he said. "There are plenty more where those came from." He rolled up the black trash bag and put it in his pocket.

"I know who you are," Daisy said. "There's a picture of you. Your first name is James."

"So you guessed it," the man said. "I wondered if you would."

"You must have the same last name as me," Daisy said, feeling more reassured by the second, "because you're a relative."

"People in the same family don't always have the same name, don't you know that?" He paused. "No, of course you don't. Why would you? My name is different from yours."

"What is it?"

He hesitated and then shrugged slightly. "It's Gritting," he said. "James Gritting."

Daisy thought Fitzjohn was a much nicer-sounding name than Gritting, but it would have been unkind of her to say that.

"Did you know my grandparents?" she asked.

"Oh, certainly," Gritting said. "Wonderful people."

He paused. "Of course Brightwood Hall was different then. Very grand. I used to think it would make a great hotel. I might have suggested the idea to your mother once or twice. Did she ever mention it?"

Daisy shook her head.

"Since then, I've changed my mind," Gritting continued. "I now think it could be so much more. The hotel would just be part of it. There's space for a golf course and a spa." He gestured over the meadow. "Cut down those big trees to make room for a parking lot . . . big indoor swimming pool . . . "

"My mum wouldn't want that," Daisy said. "This is our home!"

"Yes," Gritting said, "yes, of course."

"We like it just the way it is," Daisy said, half surprised by her fierce tone of voice.

Gritting looked at her with his head to one side, his eyes thoughtful. "I tell you what," he said. "I used to come here every summer. But I bet there are areas that even I've never seen. How about you show me around? Give me a tour of the place."

Daisy hesitated. "All right," she said at last. She looked down at her bare feet. She was still wearing her pajamas. "I'll have to have breakfast and get changed first."

"Take your time," Gritting said. "I'll be right here, waiting."

Daisy went back inside and fetched herself a bowl of cereal. Tar was nowhere to be seen. He was probably still recovering from his illness of the night before. She ate standing up at the sink, watching Gritting through the window. He had fetched the shears and was passing time by snipping and slicing at the weeds again.

I must tell him to stop doing that, Daisy thought. *It will be easier now that I know who he is.* She rinsed her cereal bowl and went upstairs to her room to get dressed.

SIXTEEN

Frank was sitting on the end of Daisy's bed. She had rolled up one sleeve of her dirty white shirt and was digging into the flesh of her arm with the tip of her knife.

"What are you doing?" Daisy said, horrified.

"Amazonian zombie tick," Frank told her with relish. "Got to get it out."

"*Zombie* tick?"

"They keep going until they get to your brain," Frank said. "Nasty way to die."

"There's no such thing as a zombie tick," Daisy said. She pulled open a drawer and started rummaging for a pair of shorts.

"You don't know much," Frank said. She dug deeper with the knife, wincing. "Even less than Sir Clarence, and that's saying something."

Daisy slammed the drawer shut with irritation. "You keep saying Sir Clarence was no good, but he must have been! He was knighted! He shot a tiger and stood on top of it!"

Frank shook her head. "Sir Clarence couldn't shoot a tiger if it was sitting on his lap."

"So who shot it, then?"

"Nobody," Frank said. "It's not really a tiger. I made it from a sack and a bit of orange paint. You don't think I'd let him kill a tiger for *real*, do you?"

She twisted the knife in her arm. "Got it!"

She pulled out the knife, wiped it clean on her trousers, and stuck it back into her belt.

"I can't spend time talking to you," Daisy said, stepping into her shorts. "I've got to show Gritting around. That's his name, James Gritting."

"What you have to do is start thinking," Frank said. "You go into the jungle with that rival explorer, you're not coming back out."

"He's not a rival explorer! He's a relative."

"Any reason why he can't be both? He broke in, didn't he? You've got no idea what he might be planning. Could be any-thing, in my opinion."

Daisy didn't reply. Frank thought the Wilderness was the Amazon jungle and Brightwood Hall was the Lost City of Valcadia. Her opinions were hardly reliable.

"Don't listen to me, then," Frank said. "Show the fellow around the place. But don't expect me to fish your bones out of the river after the piranhas are done with you."

"Everything you say is completely made up!" Daisy burst out.

Frank shrugged. "Suit yourself. Do what you want."

Daisy hesitated. "Maybe I ought to follow True's advice," she said. "He told me to go outside and look for help."

"And leave the Lost City undefended?"

"So what *should* I do?"

Frank began counting on her fingers. "Number one: secure the place. You don't want him getting inside. Number two: find a good spot for a base camp. Number three: gather provisions. Number four: you've got to find out everything you can about this Gritting fellow."

"How am I meant to do that?"

"Go find some relics," Frank said. She cast her eyes around her with a disapproving look. "Lord knows this place is full of them."

"Relics?"

"You know, pots, mummies, hieroglyphics, old tablets, anything with mysterious writing on it. Stuff that holds clues to the past. Sir Clarence is very fond of relics."

"You mean like the monkey vase on my grandfather's old desk?"

Frank snorted. "That thing? That's no relic! Sir Clarence found it in a cave in Africa. Thought it must be priceless. He hadn't noticed they were selling hundreds of the things in the market down the road. Two pence each!" She smiled scornfully. "And that was *before* haggling."

Daisy reached under her bed, where she had placed the envelope with the smashed watch. "Do you think this could be a relic?" she asked.

"It looks like one," Frank said, glancing at it. "Has it got mysterious writing on it?"

Daisy turned the watch over and looked at the inscription. "No," she said. "I can read it just fine."

"Well, it's probably still a relic," Frank said. "It's old, isn't it?"

Daisy didn't reply. She had just remembered something her mum had told her. James Gritting used to visit Brightwood Hall every summer. Then he had stopped coming and there had been a reason for that.

He stole a watch. Or they thought he had.

Daisy stared at the watch in her hand, frowning. "How did

it end up in one of Mum's Day Boxes from just a few months ago?" she asked.

But Frank had gone. Daisy was just talking to an empty space on the bed.

SEVENTEEN

Frank's talk about piranhas was all nonsense, of course, although some of her advice made sense. She had told Daisy to secure the place, which was another way of telling her to lock up the house. Daisy thought she might as well do this at once, just to be on the safe side.

She went downstairs and made sure the key was turned in the kitchen door. There was a bolt at the top of the door, and she stood on tiptoe and drew it back. She looked around the kitchen, thinking. There was a storage unit, with a chopping block built into the top, that looked heavy. Daisy leaned her whole body against it and shoved it inch by inch until it was wedged against the door.

She made her way through the Marble Hall to have another look at the front door. The wood was so thick, she thought it would take a battering ram to get it open.

Of course, a house the size of Brightwood Hall had more than two entrances. But Daisy didn't think she needed to worry too much about the others. One was in the ballroom and had been covered up behind furniture for as long as she could remember. Another led out from the library onto a patio with a view of the lake. You could turn the handle on the inside, but you couldn't push it open because it was blocked on the outside by a pile of bricks and old masonry that had been left over from a long-ago building project. There was a third door located in the back of the house, in the old utilities room. But it was made of some kind of metal—steel perhaps. The metal had rusted and jammed the lock. Daisy had tried opening it once and it hadn't given an inch.

There wasn't any way that Gritting could get into the house without a huge effort. Daisy went back upstairs.

"You forgot something!" Little Charles piped up as she walked past.

He stared at her from his nook, his eyes bright with triumph. "What?"

"You locked everything up so he can't get in," Little Charles said. "How are *you* going to get out?"

"Has anyone ever told you that you're an annoying little boy?" Daisy said.

"They wouldn't dare. They'd be flogged."

"The olden days sound horrible," Daisy said.

"Oh no," Little Charles corrected her, "they were *great*."

Daisy went back to her bedroom. Little Charles was right; she needed a secret way to get in and out of the house. After a few moments of thought, she went downstairs again to the utilities room and hunted among the old tools and laundry baskets until she found a long length of rope.

Frank might have an impressive survival bag, but Brightwood Hall was even better. It contained everything a person might ever need.

She returned to her bedroom and opened the window that faced the western side. Brightwood Hall was constructed a little like a cake, or rather several cakes, with each floor forming a new layer and a series of flat roofs and balconies connecting one part of the house with another. Directly below her window was one such area of rooftop; flat and wide, it led along the side of the building and around to the front. It was edged with a stone parapet decorated with ornamental urns.

Daisy climbed out her window, and then tied the length

of rope to the parapet. It didn't reach all the way down to the ground, although a stretch of ivy growing on the wall covered the rest of the distance. She gave the rope a tug to make sure it was secure. As a way in and out of the house it would do nicely.

Daisy walked around the side of the roof to the front of the building. It was sheltered from the breeze up there, and the sun felt warm on her face. She stood at the edge, staring out at the view. She could see so far. The broad expanse of lawn spread before her, divided by the driveway. To the left was the topiary, with True in the center like a green flag. And far beyond, behind the woodland and the wall, she could see the road. She had never noticed how it curved like that, nor that just before it did so, there was a signpost and another road . . .

She turned to look at Brightwood Hall rising at her back. From this vantage point, the walls seemed almost frighteningly close. Fast moving clouds were traveling across the sky, making the towers and turrets and ornate chimneys appear to shift and tilt towards her. Daisy reached out a hand to steady herself against one of the stone urns on the parapet. She looked down.

Gritting was standing directly below her. She could see the skin of his head through his thin hair. He must have grown tired of trimming the plants, although the shears still dangled from his hand, their blades almost long enough to reach the ground.

Daisy shrank back behind the urn, immediately aware of

two things. The first was that despite Frank's warnings and the disturbing puzzle of the watch, she had still been considering showing Gritting around the place. The second was the sudden realization that she absolutely would not do that. Seeing Gritting below, so still, so clearly waiting for her, all her fears had returned.

Gritting looked up and saw her peering around the side of the urn.

"What are you doing up there?"

"Nothing," Daisy said.

He swung the shears idly from one hand to the other, his eyes still fixed on her. "Are you ready for the tour?"

"I've changed my mind," Daisy said.

"Why?"

"I don't want to," she said. She forced herself to look him in the eyes. "I want you to go away."

Gritting made a face and spread his arms.

"You know I can't do that," he said in a kindly tone.

"Why not?"

Daisy didn't like the way he smiled, his eyes squinting against the light.

"Because I have to take care of you," he said.

EIGHTEEN

Daisy was glad now that she had already locked up the house. What else had Frank told her to do? Find a good spot for a base camp and get provisions. Daisy thought her bedroom would make a good base camp. She could exit the house through the window and use the rope to get down to the ground. She went to the basement and filled a bag with tins of food, packages of cookies, bottled water, and other necessities, and stashed it under her bed along with a can opener, binoculars, a flashlight, and several extra batteries.

She sat on the floor for a long time, with her back up against the bed, thinking about what she should do next. While she thought, she practiced her knife throwing. A stain on the baseboard of the opposite wall provided a target, although she had to throw the knife at least twenty times before she finally hit it.

Frank had suggested she look for relics. Things that might give her more information about James Gritting. The watch was a relic. Perhaps there were more like it among the thousands of Day Boxes.

The Portrait Gallery was growing shadowy. As Daisy approached the General, she turned her head sharply away. Over the past few days, her fear of him had blossomed into something closer to terror. Perhaps it was because if she looked at the General, she felt sure he would start to talk.

You're going to die! Every last one of you! he would say, and then his mouth would curve into a terrible grin.

Daisy cupped her hand to shield her face from the General's gaze and hurried past.

Halfway down the stairs, she heard a clinking noise and paused, her eyes sweeping over the Marble Hall. It was only Tar. He was scuttling precariously along the stretch of chain that ran from the pulley wheel above the chandelier all the way to the far side of the hall. He often took this shortcut, although Daisy had told him a hundred times that it was too dangerous. Tar never listened. Daisy held her breath until she saw him safely reach the end of the chain and disappear from view.

She continued downstairs and entered the dark maze of the shelving units. It smelled of old paper and dust in there, and something else: the faint lingering scent of her mother's perfume. Daisy gazed around her at the ranks of Day Boxes, each with its date written in black ink on the side.

She wondered where she should start. She opened the box closest to her. It was dated a little over a year ago. Inside there was a pink shirt—clean and folded—that Daisy had grown out of, a peacock tail feather, a tiny tin that used to hold peppermints, and a book. Whenever Daisy's mum finished reading a book, she always placed it in the box for that day. That was why there were so many gaps in the library shelves.

Daisy pushed the box back and opened another one: a pencil sketch of a bowl of fruit, an essay Daisy had written about a king called Henry, a beaded necklace, a newspaper clipping, a purple ribbon . . .

Everything held a memory, Daisy's mum had told her. Now, staring at these items, Daisy didn't understand how this could be true. The Day Boxes didn't hold anything except random objects.

She looked through five or six more. There was nothing interesting in any of them.

You couldn't put memories into boxes. It was impossible. Memories existed only in your head.

It was yet another thing that she'd always known, but never really thought about. Not until Gritting had arrived. He had made her question everything. And the more she tried to dismiss what he had said, or wish his words away, the louder they sounded in her head.

You mean you've never been out?

All this stuff piled up . . .

Crazy.

Daisy shook her head and turned away. It might be a better idea to look for relics in a different area of the maze. Perhaps towards the center, where the boxes were older and the dates on them written in a childish hand. She crept deeper through the gloom until the shelves opened into the clearing below the chandelier.

Her mum had made these Day Boxes when she was a kid. Daisy walked along slowly, examining them. She reached up on tiptoe and pulled one from a shelf above her head. It was dated twenty-five years ago. Daisy did the math in her head. Her mum would have been just ten years old. Nearly the same age as Daisy was now.

She opened the lid and reached inside.

A skipping rope, a pinecone, the label from a jar of jam, an envelope filled with pencil shavings, a paperback copy of *Treasure Island* with its pages curling up.

It gave Daisy a strange feeling to think of her mum as a kid. Daisy knew about the past because she studied history. But this felt different from learning about kings and queens, Romans and Egyptians. They were more like stories than anything else. This was real.

She replaced the items carefully in the box and reached for another.

A bottle of glittery blue nail polish, an eraser in the shape of a panda, a comb, and an envelope addressed to her mum.

Daisy recognized the handwriting. It was the same as on the envelope that held the watch: the dots above the *i*'s and the *j*'s made too large and written with the pen pressed hard against the paper. Inside the envelope was a piece of paper. Daisy unfolded it.

Dusk had fallen while she had been searching. It was now too dark in the maze to read without a light. Daisy reached in her pocket for her flashlight, her hand shaking slightly, making the bright halo dance and jerk over the paper.

There was no doubt about it. This was definitely what Frank would call a relic. Daisy read:

Dear Caroline,

You are ten now and may not remember me. I used to visit Brightwood Hall every single summer.

132

I'm your cousin James.

Actually, I'm the only real relative you still have, apart from your grandmother. Which makes what I'm about to tell you even more wrong and unfair.

The words *wrong* and *unfair* had been underlined several times.

Your grandmother hasn't let me visit since the accident. First she wouldn't return my phone calls, and then she told me to my face I wasn't welcome. She never liked me—that's the truth.

But coming to Brightwood was the best part of my whole life. I lived in a crummy little house and I went to a crummy little school, and the only thing that kept me going was the knowledge that I was related to the great Fitzjohn family and would soon be back.

I knew Brightwood was where I really belonged.

My mother tells me I'm an adult now and should just let it go. She doesn't understand.

Brightwood Hall is mine too! You understand, don't you, Caroline? If you tell your grandmother you want me to visit, she'll say okay. She does whatever you want, doesn't she? SO TELL HER!

I'm relying on you. Remember that.

James

DAY FIVE

NINETEEN

Daisy slept badly and awoke shivering in the middle of the night, even though she was under several blankets. She got up and opened a tin of peaches from her store under the bed and ate them staring out at the dark lake. Wind agitated the surface of the water and made the trees around it sway. The sky was no longer clear. She could see the huge shadows of clouds rushing to smother the moon. But there was enough light to glimpse the outline of the boathouse and the rowboat tied up in front of it.

Gritting was there for another night. There must have been plenty of food and other provisions in the bags he had taken from his car. Frank was right—he had come prepared.

When dawn finally arrived, Daisy went downstairs. Tar scurried past her down the corridor that led to the kitchen.

"How are you feeling today?" she asked him.

"Same as I always do," Tar said. "Hungry."

"You mustn't eat so much," Daisy scolded. "Look what happened to you the other day! You got sick from eating too much, didn't you?"

Tar was silent.

"Well, didn't you?"

"Something, something, something," Tar said.

Daisy was about to insist that he give her a proper answer, when she was interrupted by a sudden shrieking of birds. She went to the window to see what had alarmed them. Nothing looked out of the ordinary. The shrieking grew louder: a cacophony of warning cries and whistles, pierced by the harsh screams of peacocks.

Daisy scrambled back down the corridor and raced across the top of the shelving in the Marble Hall. Once upstairs, she went into her grandfather's old study and crawled through the furniture until she got to the window, where she could see the entire front of the estate.

Gritting was on the lawn. He was a hundred yards away, walking towards the house. Two rabbits dangled limply from his belt.

Daisy cried out and covered her mouth with her hand.

Her rabbits!

They were surely dead. Their heads bounced against Gritting's leg as he walked, and even from this distance, Daisy could see they were covered in blood. He must have set traps in the long grass near their warren.

Maybe they were the very same rabbits she had fed by hand. She had made them trusting, easy to catch. Gritting may have set the traps, but it was still her fault.

Daisy turned and crawled frantically back the way she had come. She was almost at the door to her grandfather's study when she saw Frank's muddy boots planted firmly among the forest of chair legs. Daisy looked up.

"Where are you going?" Frank asked.

"He's killing the animals!" Daisy cried. "I have to stop him!"

"How do you think you're going to do *that*?"

Daisy scrambled to her feet. She expected Frank to be right there in front of her. But the girl had vanished. Daisy whirled around. Frank was now standing on top of her grandfather's desk with one foot on the monkey vase as if it were a football that she was about to send hurtling into the air.

"I told you he was a rival explorer," she was saying in her usual bossy tone of voice. "That's what explorers always do. They arrive in a place and start killing animals. Then they make the heads into trophies and stick them on the walls of their homes to impress their guests."

Daisy didn't think the heads of her poor rabbits would impress anyone, but she had given up trying to argue with Frank.

"I have to stop him," she repeated.

"What you have to do is use your head."

"What if he kills more rabbits? Or my lovely peacocks? He called them 'vermin.' He said something had to be done about them."

Daisy's voice trembled. She held her breath, struggling against tears. She didn't want Frank to see her cry again.

"Look," Frank said in a kinder tone. "You've improved your knife-throwing skills, I'll give you that. But you're still missing more times than you hit. If it came to a fight, you wouldn't have a chance against that fellow. Better to lie low and make a plan. It's got to be a good one because it's time for you to get real. It's not like—"

Daisy had stopped listening to her. The sheer nerve of Frank telling her to "get real" pushed everything else out of her mind for a moment or two.

"How's the relic hunting by the way?" Frank asked. She had removed her foot from the monkey vase and now sat on the edge of the desk, her legs dangling.

Daisy rummaged in her pocket for the letter she had found.

"There's this," she said, holding it up so Frank could see it over the top of the furniture.

"That's a relic all right," Frank said, squinting at the words. "Hard to read though. Ancient Greek if I'm not mistaken."

Daisy bit her lip in irritation. "I can read it just fine!"

"I'm impressed," Frank said.

"I can read it because it's in English! It's a letter written to my mum when she was about my age," Daisy said. "I found something else too." She reached into her pocket again and pulled out a newspaper clipping, folded several times. "I saw this in a different, much more recent box, just before I found the letter to my mum. I noticed it had handwriting on it, although I didn't pay it any attention at the time. After I read the letter, I went back and had another look at it."

The newspaper clipping was short, with the headline MISSING BUSINESSMAN FOUND IN RAVINE.

A single paragraph followed. It was about a man who lived in a city called Brisbane. He had died falling off a cliff. He had owned several hotels, but he had been accused of something called *fraudulent business practices*. According to the writer of the newspaper article, this made some people think that perhaps he had killed himself.

Daisy had no idea what any of this meant, or even where Brisbane was located. But there were two words neatly penned in the space at the bottom of the clipping, and Daisy recognized the handwriting: *Accidents happen!*

"Why would James Gritting have written that on a bit of newspaper?" Daisy asked Frank. "And why would my mum have put it into a Day Box?"

Frank's eyes narrowed in thought. "Can I be perfectly honest?"

Daisy nodded.

"I have absolutely no idea," Frank said.

TWENTY

Daisy spent the rest of the morning in her bedroom, lying low, as Frank had advised. Every so often, she went over to the window to see if Gritting had taken the rowboat back across the lake to the boathouse. But it remained tied up at the nearby jetty. Which meant he was probably still somewhere on the main grounds.

She wondered what he was doing. Cutting the heads off the wild roses and the hollyhocks with his shears perhaps. Or laying more traps. Or tying another rabbit to his belt. He could be doing all these things while she hid like a coward in her room.

How many animals would be hanging off him by the time he was done?

Daisy pushed the thought away, but it kept returning. Each time it did, another imaginary corpse was added to Gritting's belt until he was wearing a whole skirt of dead creatures, their heads bobbing and bouncing as he strode triumphantly along.

By noon, Daisy couldn't bear it any longer. She decided to go out and see what was happening.

She let herself down the rope from her bedroom window, using the ivy to clamber down the last twenty feet, her binoculars bumping against her chest, her knife hooked to her waistband.

She turned left and crept around to the front of the house, keeping to the shadows. When she got to the corner, she stopped and scanned the lawn with her binoculars.

There was nothing there. Just the ancient trees and the grass and the shimmer of gnats in the hot air.

Daisy decided to make a wide sweep of the front grounds. She went all the way down to the gates and then back up the other side, keeping close to the perimeter wall. There was no sign of Gritting anywhere. She slipped into the topiary and paused to rest in True's cool shadow.

"How am I going to stop him, True?" she asked. "What can I do?"

The breeze shifted and it seemed the horse turned his head slightly towards her.

"I told you before," True said. "You must leave. You must get help."

"I can't," Daisy said. "I have to stay to protect the animals." She stroked his leaves. "Besides, what if I'm gone for ages and there's nobody here to trim you?"

"I grow so slowly," the horse said. "It saved me once."

He was right. When the gardeners had stopped caring for the topiary, the outlines of the other creatures had quickly been lost. But even when he was a small bush, True had never grown as well or as quickly as the others.

"It must have been terrible to see them all go," she murmured. True paused as if lost in memory.

"The worst thing was their voices," he said at last. "They got more and more muffled. And then they stopped sounding like voices any longer. I was glad when they fell silent in the end, although it almost broke my heart."

"I wish I could ride you far away," Daisy said. "I wish—"

She was interrupted by the faint crunch of gravel. She turned her head. Through the rusty, weed-strangled metal forms of the dead topiary animals she could see Gritting coming down the path by the side of the walled gardens. He was carrying the shears, and the long steel blades glittered in the sunlight with a gleam so sharp it hurt the eye.

Daisy shrank against True's side. "He's not turning," she whispered. "He's coming right towards us."

"*Hide!*" True said in a voice she had never heard before. "*Do it! Now!*"

She fell to the ground and scrambled towards the form of the baby elephant, fifteen feet away. It was covered in weeds and knotted vines. She pushed her way through and crept into the hollow cavity of its belly with her knees pressed to the earth and her head bowed.

The sound of crunching gravel stopped. Gritting had moved off the path into the ragged weeds and grass. She heard the shears: the grating whisper of the blades opening, the sharp, silvery hiss as they closed.

He's not interested in gardening, Daisy thought. *He just likes to destroy things.*

She remembered the way the long ears of the rabbits had swayed as they hung upside down, and she curled tight in her small cave, her heart hammering against the even smaller cave of her chest, her eyes squeezed shut.

The snip of the shears came again, closer than before.

A memory came to Daisy of an afternoon a long time ago, when she was tiny. She was playing hide-and-seek with her mother, sitting in the long grass of the meadow with her hands covering her eyes.

There's my baby girl! her mother had called, laughing in that soft way of hers. *Just because you've got your eyes closed it doesn't mean I can't see you!*

Another slice of the shears, so close she could hear Gritting grunt with effort as he brought the blades together. He muttered something to himself and stepped back. Daisy could feel the vibrations of his footsteps through the dry earth, loud as he passed her hiding place, then growing fainter as he moved away, through the copse of trees towards the front of the house.

She stayed where she was for several minutes, fearful he would turn and come back. Then, when she was quite sure he had gone, she crept out of the shelter of the baby elephant, brushing the earth and dried grass off her clothes.

"I think it's okay," she told True. "I think we're safe. I'll just wait here a bit longer." She sat down at his feet, gazing at his silhouette outlined against the sky. It seemed to quiver for an instant.

"True?"

There was a creaking, snapping noise. The sky turned dark and tilted towards her. The next moment, she was lying half buried beneath True's branches.

"*True!*" Daisy cried, scrambling to her feet.

He lay on his side, his central stem cut almost completely in two. Gritting's shears had managed to sever all except a thin strand of bark. The horse had held himself upright as the blades bit deep and for long moments after, through balance or through force of will. Now, at last he had given way.

He looked different on the ground. His legs no longer looked like legs. They were just an undignified collection of spindly branches. Daisy touched his head. His eyes were closed.

He had been made into a horse by chance. Nothing but chance had preserved him through the long, lonely years of neglect. And now a random snip of the shears had brought him down.

"It's not important." His voice was as thin as a reed. "None of that matters. In the end, the only thing that matters is to keep your Shape . . . "

She stroked his nose and his ragged, leafy ears.

"Please," she begged. "Please don't go."

He didn't reply.

"Does it hurt?" she asked.

"I thought it would," True said. "But it doesn't. It's strange, like being . . . untied."

Daisy examined his poor broken stem. "I could try and tie it back together," she cried. "Or fetch water. Would it help if you had water?"

He was silent. Not even his leaves rustled.

"Be careful of yourself," he said at last. She had to lower her head close to hear him.

"Will you be able to run, where you're going?" she whispered. "Will you gallop?"

He didn't answer.

Daisy sat beside him for a long while. She had cried many times in the past few days, but she didn't cry now. It felt as though she couldn't, even if she tried. At last, she got up and made her way slowly back to the house.

TWENTY-ONE

Daisy crept into her mum's room, desperate for comfort. It was the closest she could get to actually being with her. But there was no comfort there. Despite the clutter, the room felt empty. Her mum's dresses hung like ghosts in the closet, and her paintings had their faces turned to the wall.

The only picture her mum had ever displayed was the portrait of Daisy hanging in the reception area, although Daisy thought her mum's paintings were beautiful.

She sat on the floor in her mum's bedroom and turned the nearest painting around so she could see it. It was another—more recent—portrait of her. She was sitting with her legs tucked up in an armchair. The chair was covered with orange velvet, so cleverly painted that it looked real enough to touch.

There was a tiny white brooch pinned to the painted collar of Daisy's shirt. Daisy leaned in for a closer look. She didn't own a brooch like that, in the shape of a boat.

Except it wasn't a boat. It was a yacht. Daisy could see the masts and the tiny wisp of a flag. It was the *Everlasting*.

Curious, she put the painting aside and looked at the next one in the stack. It showed a bowl of fruit on a table and, next to it, a bunch of daffodils in a tall glass vase. The bowl was decorated with blue and white squares. It looked exactly like the one downstairs in the kitchen, although now, examining it more carefully, Daisy saw there was one tiny difference. Her mum had painted the shape of the yacht in one of the white squares.

"The *Everlasting*," Daisy whispered.

She looked at other pictures, slowly at first, and then more and more rapidly. There were at least fifteen years' worth of paintings, stacked in groups of ten, all of them showing some aspect of Brightwood Hall. There were portraits of Daisy in different stages of her life, scenes of the house, the gardens, and a whole variety of familiar objects.

The *Everlasting* was in every single picture.

Sometimes it was plain to see. In one painting, for example, it appeared as an ornament on the ballroom mantelpiece. In another, it was a toy lying among Daisy's dolls and books. But mostly, the yacht was hard to find, hiding in the shape of a cloud or woven into the pattern of a carpet.

Her mum hardly ever mentioned the accident that had destroyed her family, and Daisy had assumed it was because she didn't think about it much. Now she saw that she had been quite wrong about this.

She turned the last picture around. It had been painted before Daisy was born. It showed the lawn and the great trees, deep in the green dream of a summer afternoon. Daisy looked for the *Everlasting*, and sure enough, she found it. A faint outline on the grass, formed from a shadow, like a trick of the light.

Her mum must have thought about it every hour of every day. She was obsessed with it.

Daisy wished that word *obsessed* hadn't come into her mind. Now it wouldn't go away. She thought of her mum's Day Boxes and the piles of groceries stacked up like protective walls.

Obsessed.

She stood up, rubbing her face in agitation, not noticing that her hands were dusty from the paintings. She saw a card lying on the floor. It must have fallen between two of the older paintings and lain forgotten until now. Daisy picked it up. There was a photograph of a kangaroo on one side and words on the other. Daisy could see at a glance that it was Gritting's handwriting.

She stuffed it into the back pocket of her shorts to read more carefully later. She was too busy with her thoughts to worry about relics just now.

The *Everlasting* had made her think about the rowboat, although apart from the fact that they both floated, the yacht and the boat were completely different. For one thing, the boat was tiny. For another, it was extremely old: the planks worn and splintery, the wood almost rotten in places.

Thinking about it gave Daisy an idea.

There was a drill among the tools in the utilities room. She went down to have a look at it. She pressed the trigger tentatively and the drill bit whirred.

There was no time to go back upstairs and exit the building using the rope. Gritting might decide to return to the boathouse at any moment. Daisy pulled the heavy storage unit away from the kitchen door and slipped outside.

She crept around the sheds to the lake and jetty and, without giving herself a chance to feel frightened, scrambled into the rowboat. It was even easier than she thought to drill into the old wood. She chose a spot underneath the seat, where Gritting wouldn't see, and drilled five holes in the bottom of the boat. It wasn't enough to let in a lot of water when the boat was empty, but Gritting's weight would turn the trickle into a flood.

"He'll sink," she told the Hunter.

"'Tis a lonely grave, beneath the waves," the Hunter commented in a dreamy voice.

"He's not going to *drown*," Daisy said. "He'll just get wet."

"Wet?" The Hunter sounded puzzled. The idea of getting wet was obviously not poetic enough for him to fully grasp.

"He'll get drenched," Daisy said, trying to be helpful.

"Ah, *drenched*," the Hunter repeated, his beautiful face lighting up. "Drenched in the lake of eternity . . . drenched in the water of—"

Daisy had already gone. She ran back to the house and pushed the storage unit up against the kitchen door again. Then she went upstairs and out onto the roof. She was just in time. Gritting was walking down the path to the lake. He turned a corner and she couldn't see him any longer. In a few seconds, he would be at the jetty.

The boat itself was beyond her line of sight, hidden by the angle of the house. She held her binoculars tight and waited.

One minute. Then two.

Had he seen the holes? Was the boat already full of water?

No. Gritting entered her vision, rowing in his lurching way. Daisy thought the boat looked lower in the water than she remembered, although she might have just been imagining it. It was nearly evening, the sun was low over the lake, and the surface of the water glittered, half blinding her.

He was twenty yards out, and now there wasn't any doubt about the boat being lower. It was barely a few inches above the water. Gritting was just a silhouette against the sun, and he had begun to row faster, his body jerking back and forth, the oars digging into the water with a frantic motion.

He tried to turn but was already at the middle of the lake. The boat was level with the surface. In another, instant it had slipped from sight. Gritting leaped to his feet. For a split second, he looked as if he were standing on nothing except water. Then he too was gone.

Daisy turned and scrambled back through her bedroom window, half terrified by what she had done. What if Gritting couldn't swim? What if he got tangled in weeds and pulled to the bottom?

She ran through the Portrait Gallery in a panic.

"I didn't mean to drown him!" she cried.

"We used to drown witches in the olden days!" Little Charles's voice was jubilant.

"I don't believe you!"

"It's true. Witches got thrown in the lake."

"Be quiet, Little Charles!"

"They were rubbish witches anyway," he said. "If they'd been any good, they'd have done a spell to make themselves invisible or dry up the lake or something. So they deserved to be drowned."

Daisy hurried past him and down the great staircase.

Tar was waiting for her in the kitchen. She hadn't fed him for a while.

"I didn't drown him, did I?" she said. "It isn't my fault, is it?"

"Something, something, something," Tar muttered, not meeting her eye. Daisy fetched some stale bread, tore it into pieces, and knelt on the floor to feed him.

"I just wanted to cut him off from the boathouse," Daisy said. "I just thought if he couldn't get to his equipment and provisions, he'd *have* to leave."

She paused. A terrible thought had just occurred to her.

"Do dead bodies float, or do they sink?" she asked Tar.

"Neither," Tar said promptly. "First they get eaten by fish. Then they drift up on the shore with lots of bits missing . . ."

"I shouldn't have done it!" Daisy wailed. "I shouldn't have—"

There was a noise outside. A rustling. She glanced up. From her vantage point on the floor, she could see the side of the sink unit and the window that looked out on the patio beyond.

It was dark outside. The noise came again. She was just about to get to her feet when she froze. Gritting's face was suddenly there, framed by the window. His wet hair hung like weeds, and the pupils of his eyes, always small, now looked as if they had been washed clean away, leaving his gaze as flat and as featureless as the lake itself.

TWENTY-TWO

Daisy screamed and scurried across the floor on her hands and knees. She heard a thudding noise. It was the sound of Gritting banging on the window. Daisy crawled into the room next to the kitchen. It was full of old cooking equipment. Dozens of copper pots and pans hung from the ceiling. She pressed herself against the side of an oven and put her hand over her mouth to stop herself from screaming again.

Gritting had stopped banging on the window. Now he was trying to get in through the kitchen door. Daisy could hear crashing as he shoved himself against it and then the slow scrape of the storage unit being pushed away.

She had made a mistake. She should have run in the opposite direction, into the tightly packed corridor that led to the Marble Hall. He wouldn't have been able to follow her in there, not without a great deal of time and effort. She could have made her way upstairs and escaped down the rope.

The room she was in had only two doors. One led back into the kitchen, the other down to the wine cellar, a dark space filled with ancient bottles stacked in dusty rows.

Daisy hesitated, wondering if she had time to double back and reach the safety of the corridor. Even as she considered it, the storage unit gave a long, last scrape against the floor, and she heard the kitchen door bang open.

Gritting had broken in.

She leaped to her feet and dashed through the door to the wine cellar. There was a key in the lock, although that was on the outside. She closed the door behind her as quietly as she could, her fingers groping for a bolt or hook. There was nothing.

She was standing at the top of a narrow flight of stairs that descended into pitch darkness, and the air was full of a musty, fruity scent. Daisy grabbed the handle of the door and held on to it as tightly as she could, trying to breathe quietly.

For a moment or two, all she could hear was the muffled thump of her own heart. Then, just as she had begun to hope that Gritting had left, she heard his footsteps in the kitchen.

The steps grew louder. He had entered the side room. She heard a clattering and a grunt of pain. He had hit his head on the copper pans, she guessed. Two or three of them rolled—or were kicked—across the floor.

Daisy's hands were slippery on the door handle. She leaned back, teetering on the edge of the top step.

The clattering died away, and Gritting's footsteps approached the door. The nearer they came, the softer and slower they seemed. He was very close now. Nothing separated them except the width of the door.

She clung desperately to the handle, knowing it was hopeless. There wasn't a chance of holding the door closed against him. She stood there for what seemed like a long time, although it wasn't much more than a second or two, waiting for the terrible feel of his grasp on the other side of the handle. It never came. Instead she heard something unexpected.

It was the sound of the key turning in the lock.

Daisy caught her breath in surprise. His steps retreated. She heard him in the kitchen and then the sound of the back door closing. She waited another minute and then pushed against the door. It was as solid as a wall.

She was locked in.

Daisy almost never went into the wine cellar. There was nothing in there to interest her. Just a lot of cobwebby bottles on shelves. Yet she had been down there often enough to know that there was no other way out of the place. Her hand crept up the wall, searching for the light cord.

The bulb hadn't been replaced in a long time. The light was dim and flickering. But now she could see down the narrow staircase to the cavern below.

She turned and banged loudly on the door. Bad as it might be to confront Gritting, it was still better than being trapped down there.

"Hey!" Daisy called. "Hey! I'm locked in!"

She listened for a moment. *"I'M LOCKED IN!"*

Nobody answered.

Daisy sat down on the top step. It was warm and airless in the cellar, and she was already feeling thirsty.

"Good thing you've got plenty to drink, then," Frank said in a sarcastic voice. She was down below, leaning casually against the nearest shelf of bottles.

"I can't drink it," Daisy said. "It'll make me sick."

"Sir Clarence drinks whiskey," Frank commented. "Once he drank a whole bottle and started running around on his knuckles."

"His knuckles?"

"He thought he was an orangutan," Frank explained. "He climbed up a baobab tree. Took me half an hour and seven bananas to get him down."

"I don't believe a single thing you say!"

"A tomb is a funny place to keep wine," Frank said, looking around her. "Who's buried here, anyway?"

"It's not a tomb—it's a wine cellar."

"Is that what you call it in Valcadia?" Frank pulled out a notebook and pencil. "Interesting . . . "

"I was only trying to make Gritting go away," Daisy said, changing the subject. "But he didn't go away. All he did was get wet."

"And very angry," she added, remembering the sight of his face at the window. Despite the warmth of the cellar, she shivered slightly.

"I'll give you points for effort," Frank said, putting her notebook away. "But it was a complete and utter failure."

Daisy didn't say anything. For once, Frank was right.

"The main thing wrong with your plan," Frank continued, "was you aimed too low. You tried to make him leave. You've got to do more than that. You've got to *defeat* him. To do that," she said casually, "you've probably got to hurt him."

"I'm not going to hurt him!" Daisy cried. "Why would I do that?"

In the dim light of the cellar, Frank's figure was half lost in shadow, her eyes no more than two dark holes. "Why not?" she said. "He's already tried to kill *you* twice."

"That's ridiculous!"

"What about the strawberries?" Frank said.

Daisy didn't answer.

"You knew your pet got sick from the strawberries," Frank continued. "You didn't want to admit it, did you?"

"That's not true!" Daisy said, pressing her hands tight between her knees. "It's not . . . " She paused, drawing a deep breath. "There's a tub of weed killer in the gardener's old shed," she said slowly. "I know he went in there. He said he was looking for tools."

"Of course he did!" Frank said. "And what about the next day, when he saw you walking around like nothing had happened? Remember what he said?"

Daisy thought of Gritting in the Winter Grove, with the black trash bag in his hand and his eyes on her face.

Didn't you enjoy the strawberries?

"He knew I hadn't eaten them!" Daisy said with a rush of horror.

"Now you get it," Frank said. "It's taken you enough time! Don't feel bad," she added in a kinder voice. "Not everyone can be clever, you know. I'm sure you have many other good qualities . . . "

"What was the other time?" Daisy said. "You said he's tried it twice. To kill me, I mean."

Frank shrugged and looked around. "He's locked you up in here, hasn't he? Thinks you can't get out."

"Maybe it was just a mistake," Daisy said. But she knew it was a feeble explanation. She had banged on the door of the wine cellar and shouted as loudly as she could. Gritting must surely have heard her.

"But it doesn't make any sense," she protested. "He could have tried to hurt me when . . . when we were drinking tea, or when we were standing outside, or anytime. He didn't have to be *sneaky* about it."

"I think he wants to make it look like an accident," Frank said. "You'll be just one more little skeleton among all the dead down here. And once you're gone, he gets to keep Valcadia all to himself."

"What am I going to do?" Daisy cried. "How am I going to get out?"

"It's a tomb, isn't it? There are always trapdoors and secret passageways in places like this. To foil tomb robbers, you know."

"There aren't any trapdoors or secret passageways!"

"Have you looked?"

"I don't have to!"

Above Daisy's head, the lightbulb made a crackling noise and then went out.

TWENTY-THREE

F rank? Are you still there?"

The wine cellar was silent. Daisy got to her feet and felt her way down the stairs, her hands groping along the wall. At the bottom, not knowing where the stairs ended, she nearly tripped, her arms flailing in the darkness.

"Please still be there," she whispered. There was no reply. The sharp, fruity smell of the wine was even stronger. Daisy stretched out her hands and took a few tiny steps forward. She felt the cool curve of glass and ran her fingers over a row of bottles. To the best of her memory, there were about five or six rows of shelves in the wine cellar, with more bottles stacked against the walls. She crept along to the end of a shelf and turned. There were bottles on either side of her now.

"Where are you?" she said.

Daisy wished that she hadn't gone down the stairs. She should have stayed at the top, where there was at least a crack of light underneath the door.

She fumbled her way towards where she thought the stairs had been and found she was blocked. She turned. She couldn't be lost. Not in a space that was barely bigger than her bedroom. The darkness had robbed her of all sense of direction. She turned again, stumbled, and grabbed at a shelf to keep from falling. Bottles tumbled around her. She heard the sound of breaking glass and felt liquid splash on her legs.

Her feet were bare. Daisy leaped back automatically to avoid cutting herself and slammed into another shelf, sending more bottles toppling. She fell hard, curling into a ball and covering her head with her hands. For a moment or two, she was aware of nothing except the crash and thunder of objects falling all around her.

If Gritting were anywhere nearby, he must surely have heard the noise. Daisy waited for the sound of the wine-cellar door opening. But it never came. She staggered to her feet, half gagging on the thick, rich smell of wine that rose all around her. The floor was covered with bits of broken glass. She turned to her right and immediately bumped into a cold wall of the cellar. She groped her way along it, hoping to find the stairs again. Instead she found something else.

It was the handle of a door.

There was a way out after all. Frank had been right.

Daisy didn't give herself a chance to worry whether the door was locked or not. She pulled the handle.

The door opened and Daisy instantly felt along the wall for a light switch. She was standing on a tiny landing with a flight of stairs leading out of sight. The stairs were extremely narrow and covered with a thick layer of dust. Although she had never seen them before, Daisy wasn't completely surprised to find them. There were many such flights of staircases in Brightwood Hall. Her mum had told her that the servants used them in the old days.

The stairs turned a corner and continued up. Daisy thought she must be on the second floor of the house by now. She reached another landing, with a door to the left and one to the right. She tried each but they were both locked.

Up and up she went, her bare feet leaving tracks in the dust. At the top, there was a corridor and a single door. Below the handle, there was the outline of a handprint in faded blue paint. It was tiny, far smaller than Daisy's own hand would have made.

She drew in her breath and opened the door. The room was

dark. Her fingers searched for the light, found it, and switched it on.

Daisy knew at once where she was because there was a garden painted on the walls. Dandelion spores drifted above the meadow and rose like stars up to the blue-sky ceiling. Around the little window, the trees were in blossom and trailing roses curled above the bed.

The room had been her mum's bedroom when she was a little girl.

Daisy entered slowly, as if her step might break something.

Her mum had awoken every morning in this little bed. She had played with the toys in the cupboard. And at night, she had gone to sleep with the moonlight casting shadows over the painted foxgloves and forget-me-nots.

The room hadn't been touched since then. It had simply been left behind.

Daisy walked over to the bed. It was still made up, although the sheets were yellow with age and a corner of one trailed in the dust. She bent to tuck it back in. There was a box underneath the bed. Daisy got down on her stomach and pulled it out.

It was just an old shoe box, not nearly as sturdy as the boxes her mum used now. But Daisy knew it was a Day Box because it had a date written on one end. Inside was a twisted handkerchief, a label from a cereal box, a plastic bracelet, and a beautiful doll. The doll was wearing a yellow dress with yellow matching shoes.

Daisy lifted her out carefully. She touched the doll's hair and ran a finger over the outlines of her face.

It was Dolly Caroline. She had been made to look exactly like Daisy's mum, with the same shape to her nose and mouth, the same beautiful gray eyes. She was so lifelike, it was almost like meeting her own mother when she had been a child. Years and years ago, long before the accident. When the topiary creatures had still been green, and there were parties in the ballroom and Brightwood Hall was filled with laughter instead of dusty boxes.

"Oh, *Mum*," Daisy said, hugging the doll tight to her heart. "Poor little Mum . . . "

All Daisy's life, her mum had taught her that if you didn't hold on to things, they would be lost. But if Dolly Caroline hadn't lost a shoe all those years before, her mum would have stayed on the *Everlasting*. She would have died with the rest of her family. And then Daisy herself would never have been born.

Maybe losing things wasn't so terrible.

Maybe some things were meant to be lost.

TWENTY-FOUR

There was another door out of her mum's bedroom. It opened onto a corridor almost completely jammed with objects and furniture. Daisy got to her knees and began to crawl through the thickets of chair legs and floor lamps, over logs of rolled-up carpets and deep into forgotten caverns beneath tables.

At one point, the way was completely blocked by several huge dressers. She couldn't climb over them because they were covered with a jumble of what looked like plates and china ornaments. And the dressers were wedged so tightly against the wall that she couldn't squeeze past.

It seemed no wonder her mum's old room had been forgotten. Nobody could reach it.

She hesitated for a second and then jumped, straddling the width of the corridor with her palms and the soles of her bare feet pressed tight against the walls. It was hard, but by bracing her arms and legs and moving quickly, she managed to keep her body suspended above the dressers while making her way to the end of the corridor before dropping to the floor again.

Daisy squeezed her aching arms and tried to figure out where she was in the house. She went along another corridor and then down a flight of stairs, and suddenly found herself at the far end of the Portrait Gallery.

She heard the clock striking. It was late. Eleven o'clock at night.

Daisy went back to her room. Her face was pale when she looked in the mirror, her hair wild around her face. She tried to tuck the strands back into her braid, but it was no use.

She looked terrible. She looked like a frightened little ghost.

Normally her mum did her hair. She used a silver-backed hairbrush that used to belong to her grandmother. She brushed and brushed until Daisy's hair fell in a satin sheet to her waist. Sometimes she sang:

Down in the valley, the valley so low,

Hang your head over, hear the winds blow . . .

Gritting for sure thought she was a frightened little ghost. Daisy clutched her braid at the nape of her neck, pulling it as tight as she could, and reached for her knife with the other hand. He thought he could get rid of her like he had gotten rid of the weeds and the rabbits.

He was wrong.

Roses love sunshine, violets love dew,

Angels in heaven know I love—

Daisy closed her eyes and cut as firmly as she could.

When she opened her eyes, she looked completely different. She didn't look frightened any longer. She looked ragged and fierce and *real*. Daisy glanced down at the long coil of her braid still hanging from her hand. Now that it wasn't a part of her anymore it looked like any other object. Something that she might not even have recognized as hers unless she had just cut it off her own head.

"That's better," Frank said from the other side of the room. "Now you look like you're ready to put up a fight. But you can't be wearing those little-kid shorts. I suggest a stout pair of jungle pants."

"Jungle pants?"

"Dark green with plenty of pockets," Frank informed her. "Plus loops for hanging things off."

Daisy went to her chest of drawers. "These are the right

color," she said, holding up a pair of trousers she wore when she helped mow the lawn. "Will these do?"

"I suppose they'll have to," Frank said, clearly unimpressed.

Daisy was changing into the trousers when she remembered the card with the kangaroo that she'd found in her mother's bedroom. It was still in the pocket of her shorts.

"I found another relic," she told Frank, pulling it out.

The kangaroo was brown, with a baby peeking out of its pouch. Underneath the photo, it said: GREETINGS FROM DOWN UNDER!

Daisy turned the card over and looked at the date. "It's from ages ago," she said. "Eleven years." Gritting had written:

Dear Caroline,

You've ignored me for a long time, but now you won't need to do it any longer! I've left the country. I'm going into the hotel business with a partner in Australia. I don't plan on coming back.

I hope you have a good life. I certainly will!

Daisy thought it was a rather nasty message, although she wasn't sure exactly why. She had felt the same about the letter

Gritting had written to her mother. As if there was something bad hiding just behind the words.

"He killed my horse," she told Frank. "Did you know that?"

Frank shook her head in disgust.

"He did it for no good reason," Daisy said. "Just for the fun of it."

"You can't trust anyone who kills things for fun," Frank commented. "They're rotten on the inside. You've got to deal with this fellow."

"That's easy for you to say," Daisy said.

"I find most things easy," Frank said.

"So how should I deal with him?"

"It's obvious," Frank said, looking smug. "So obvious, even you should get it."

Daisy thought that real or not, Frank was begging to be kicked.

"So tell me!"

Frank folded her arms across her chest and tilted her head to one side in a patronizing manner. "I'll make this simple. Lost cities always have temples in them, don't they? And what do temples have?"

Daisy stared at her blankly.

Frank sighed. "They have *traps*! Floors that slide open, knives that come out of the wall—that kind of thing. All you have to do is lure this rival explorer into the temple and wait for him to get caught."

Daisy was furious with herself for believing—even for a moment—that Frank might have anything useful to suggest. "That's completely ridiculous!" she snapped.

"Where's the fellow now?" Frank said, ignoring her. "Thanks to you, he can't get back across the river because you destroyed his boat. Which means he could be . . . anywhere."

"I think he's in the room above the garage," Daisy said. "The lights are on up there. He must be staying there for the night."

"Good," Frank said. "That gives us time. It's still hours to morning."

"I don't even *have* a temple!" Daisy burst out.

"Then you'd better hurry up and find one," Frank said.

TWENTY-FIVE

Daisy didn't dare to switch on the chandelier in the Marble Hall in case Gritting was still awake. There was a clear view of the house from the room above the garage, and she didn't want him to look out and see her. Instead she put on a couple of lights that stood on a table near the entrance to the ballroom.

In the dim glow of these lights, the Marble Hall *did* look a little like a temple. The shelves cast long shadows like columns, and the area beneath the chandelier was just where an altar might go.

"Rival explorers always enter the temple sooner or later," Frank told her from a spot above her head.

Daisy glanced up. She was sitting cross-legged on top of one of the shelving units. "They're so greedy for artifacts and relics and treasure and stuff, they don't bother to take care."

Frank ran a finger across her grimy neck. "Next thing you know, it's all over," she said with relish. She looked around hopefully. "Any trapdoors in here? Arrows triggered by a hidden lever?"

Daisy shook her head. But she was busy thinking. In this shadowy light, the thousands of Day Boxes looked a lot like stone blocks.

She would need a ladder. There was one in the utilities room. But Daisy knew it would be impossible to move it through all the clutter in the corridors. Luckily there was a stepladder in the reception area. It was tall enough.

The stepladder made a terrible clattering noise as she half dragged, half carried it over to the first row of shelving. Every few moments, she stopped, her heart pounding, as she wondered whether Gritting could hear the commotion from the garage.

The shelves had been positioned close together to allow the maximum amount of storage space. And what made the pathways between them even narrower was the fact that the Day Boxes were longer than the width of the shelving, so they stuck out on either side. If the boxes weren't there, even a large person might make their way through.

Even a person as large as James Gritting.

Daisy pulled out a Day Box and rested it on the stepladder. Then she hesitated. She was allowed to look through her mum's things, although not to move the boxes. The boxes were arranged by date. If she started shifting them around, they would get out of order. And what she was planning to do was far, far worse than simply getting a few boxes out of order.

But the boxes took up so much space. All the days gone by piled one upon the other. Soon they would fill the house until there wasn't space left for any new days at all. There would be room only for the past.

Without giving herself a chance to change her mind, Daisy quickly pulled out another box. She carried both boxes up the stepladder and set them down on top of the shelving unit. Then she went down for another pair.

It was hot, sweaty work. Daisy could carry only two boxes at a time, and even then, she had to stop every few minutes to catch her breath. The ladder creaked and lurched as she went up and down, and several times, her hands slipped and boxes fell to the ground. They broke open and objects scattered across the floor. Daisy hurried to pick them up.

"You haven't got time for that," Frank reminded her. "How many blocks have you got so far?"

Daisy made a quick count. "Nearly thirty."

"Not enough." Frank frowned. "You need *a lot* more than that for a decent trap."

After a couple of hours of effort, Daisy had removed most of the boxes from a single avenue of shelving. Now that there was more room, the boxes that were left could be repositioned so they didn't stick out on either end. She shoved them into place with aching arms. Her throat felt tight. Moving the boxes had dislodged years of dust. She saw it rising like smoke in the weak light.

"Incense," Frank said, nodding to herself. "Temples always have plenty of incense." She got up from her perch and walked slowly along the top of the shelving units, staring at Daisy's handiwork with a critical eye.

"He'll be able to get into this part of the temple now," Frank said. "But it isn't enough. You want him turning the corner. He's got to be able to get to the middle."

"I'm tired," Daisy said. "I need to eat."

She went to the kitchen and opened a package of cookies, suddenly starving. She ate them two at a time, standing at the sink to catch the crumbs. Tar was at her side at the first rustle of the packaging.

"I should give you something better to eat," she said, tossing him a corner of a cookie. "But I don't have time to cook anything. I've got to get Gritting into the temple and then trap him."

Tar appeared to shiver slightly at the word "trap." "What are you going to do with him after that?"

Daisy thought of the knife in her belt. She had gotten much better at throwing it. Now she could almost always hit a target without taking more than a second or two to aim.

"What would *you* do, Tar?"

The rat made a dart for a cookie crumb and stuffed it into his mouth. "Something, something, something," he mumbled.

Daisy returned to the Marble Hall. She needed to clear additional passageways to lead Gritting deeper into the maze of shelving units, so deep he couldn't easily escape from her trap.

She took a deep breath and went back to work.

It was three in the morning before Daisy had cleared another passageway and nearly dawn by the time there was a way through the maze to the central area below the chandelier. The tops of the shelving units were piled high with the Day Boxes she'd removed, and movement up there had become difficult.

"You'll have to arrange them better than that," Frank told her.

Daisy gritted her teeth. "I *know*! I'm the one doing all the work, remember?" She stared at the boxes. They needed to be set up in such a way that she could send them tumbling with only a shove or two. After a bit of thought, she chose a place close to the central clearing where the tops of three shelves joined together to form a T. This would give her enough room to get behind the pile of boxes when the time came to push them down.

Daisy stacked them carefully, one on top of the other, with their ends sticking out over the side of the shelf so that they would fall forward into the passageway below. Even though she had cleared the passageway, it was still narrow, and she thought fifty or sixty boxes would block it completely. The first light of morning was creeping through the Marble Hall by the time Daisy was done. She sat at the top of the great staircase, gazing down at her work.

Gritting would enter the twisting path below. He would follow it all the way to the clearing beneath the chandelier. Then Daisy would push the Day Boxes down behind him, blocking his exit.

It was quiet in the Marble Hall. The only movement came from Tar taking his usual shortcut along the chain that looped from the back wall all the way up to the ceiling pulley wheel that held the chandelier in place. For once, Daisy was too tired to scold him as he disappeared from view.

Daisy closed her eyes. Her hair was full of dust and her hands were black with dirt. She didn't care. She had made what was probably one of the best temple traps in the history of the world.

The only question was: how was she going to get James Gritting inside?

DAY SIX

TWENTY-SIX

Daisy rested her head against the bannister and waited for the sun to rise a little higher. Soon, Gritting would be up. She would wash her face and hands and brush her hair, and then she would go and find him. Getting him into the maze wouldn't be hard at all, she decided. She wouldn't need any kind of trick.

She would merely invite him in.

Gritting might suspect Daisy was responsible for sinking the rowboat, although he couldn't be sure. Which meant she wouldn't have to explain anything or even mention the incident. She would only have to pretend she had changed her mind about showing him around the place.

I'm so sorry I was rude to you, she would tell him. *I didn't mean it, I was scared. Would you like to have another cup of tea?*

It all seemed simple in the quiet of the Marble Hall, with the long shafts of morning light full of the slow swirl of dust. But just as Daisy was starting to believe that she had nothing to feel frightened about, she heard the sound of footsteps on the gravel driveway outside, and her calm was instantly replaced by terror.

He was outside.

Daisy shot to her feet. Her first instinct was to run away and hide, but instead she took a deep breath, crept down the staircase to the front door, and peered cautiously outside.

Gritting was standing on the driveway. His trousers appeared still damp from his dunking in the lake, and his thin hair was awry. He looked as if his night had been uncomfortable.

Daisy remembered the sound of the key turning in the lock on the wine cellar door and the way Tar had nearly died after licking the strawberries. Anger made her brave. She took a step forward, out of the shadows.

"Hey!"

Gritting jerked with shock. It might have been the surprise of how different she looked: her hair cut short, her expression fierce. But Daisy felt certain it was because he thought she was still where he had left her, locked up in the wine cellar.

He stared at her speechlessly for a second or two, and then his shoulders seemed to relax.

"There you are," Gritting said. He shrugged and half turned away. "I wondered whether I'd see you before I left."

"What do you mean?" Daisy said.

Gritting shrugged again and began to walk slowly towards his car on the far side of the driveway. "You told me you wanted me to leave. So I'm leaving."

Daisy felt confused. This wasn't how she had planned things. She was supposed to be inviting Gritting inside so she could trap him in the maze. But now it seemed that none of that would be needed after all.

He reached the door of his car, opened it, and then paused, shaking his head in a sorrowful fashion. "I was only trying to be helpful," he said in a sad voice.

"You weren't!" Daisy burst out. "You were trying to—"

Gritting leaned on the door, looking at her. "You must have a very low opinion of me," he said in the same sad voice. "But I've only had your best interests at heart."

"You tried to poison me with those strawberries!" Daisy cried. "Tar nearly died."

"I did *what*?"

"And then you left me to starve in the wine cellar!"

Gritting stared at her with wide-open, disbelieving eyes. "I thought you'd *like* the strawberries," he said. "They were perfectly fine. Don't you think it's more likely that your pet ate something else that made him sick?"

Daisy didn't answer.

"As for the wine cellar," Gritting continued, "I do remember locking the door. It's extremely dangerous to have all that alcohol lying around where children can get to it. But I certainly didn't know you were down there!"

He had an explanation for everything. Was it possible he was telling the truth?

"What about my rabbits?" she said. "You can't say you didn't kill the rabbits."

Gritting sighed. "It's true. I did kill them, although they didn't feel a thing." He paused. "I don't know how I can make you understand, but this place used to be so different. Your mother has let it go to a terrible degree. The animals may look harmless, but they're destroying the grounds. I was simply trying to clear the place. For old times' sake, you know."

He sounded sincere, almost sorry. Yet no matter what he said, Daisy knew she would never like him.

"I was only trying to be helpful," Gritting repeated. "But I can see I'm not wanted."

He hesitated, as if waiting for an apology. Daisy kept her

mouth tight shut. Gritting shook his head and got into his car. He turned on the engine.

Daisy watched him go, the car bumping down the driveway. At the end, the car stopped and she saw him get out and open the gates before driving through and out of sight. She waited for several minutes to make sure he was truly gone before she allowed herself to finally relax.

Gritting had left. The house was hers again. But behind the relief, a small detail nagged at her. A feeling of wrongness, of something being missing. Daisy had no idea what it was. Only that it seemed important.

Daisy turned and went back into the house, still thinking about it.

TWENTY-SEVEN

Daisy stared at herself in her bedroom mirror. She ought to have felt happy—even triumphant—about Gritting leaving Brightwood Hall. But she didn't look happy. She looked worried.

Gritting had left, but Daisy still didn't know what had happened to her mum, or whether she was ever coming back. And she hadn't done anything to try to find out. Instead she had spent the days talking to a girl who wasn't there and imagining that someone was plotting to hurt her.

Daisy fingered the nape of her neck, tugging at her short hair. She didn't look fierce at all. She looked like a little girl playing dress-up.

Lying on the bed with her body curled tight, Daisy wondered what she should do. She could always stay where she was, waiting and hoping for her mother to return.

What if her mum never came back? Daisy thought of time passing, the seasons turning, and herself changing and getting older, without a living person to talk to or anyone to know or care whether she existed or not. The idea was so lonely and terrifying that Daisy had to bury her face in the pillow to stop herself from bursting into tears.

Daisy couldn't stay. She should have left days ago, when True first told her to go. Daisy thought of him lying on his side, his green leaves already withering, his body growing brittle in the sun. If he could still talk, he would tell her again to leave. At once, this minute.

But she was so tired. She closed her eyes, comforted by the familiar sounds of the old house. She would rest today and leave in the morning, when she was fresh.

Daisy wondered what it would be like to be somewhere else. To be in a place where you didn't instantly recognize every creak and rustle and clank of the building . . .

She sat up straight, all thoughts of leaving abruptly forgotten.

She knew what had been nagging at her ever since Gritting had left. The sound of his car had been wrong.

Daisy knew every noise in Brightwood Hall. Every faulty

piece of plumbing, every snatch of birdsong. She knew the noise her mum's car made too. It sounded loud on the driveway. By the time it reached the main gates, it was just a low hum. Yet on a calm day like this one, you could still hear it for a while on the road beyond, a distant insect buzz growing fainter and fainter until it was gone.

The noise of Gritting's car hadn't grown fainter and fainter. It had just stopped.

There was only one place in Brightwood Hall where you could see more than a short stretch of the road outside. Daisy ran to her bedroom window, scrambled out, and hurried around the corner to the front area of roof. The sun was already high, and beneath her bare feet, the stone was hot, almost burning. She stood at the edge of the roof and looked down over the lawn and meadow to the gates beyond. From here, she could see where the road outside curved and ran a little way until it reached an intersection with another road.

Almost at the intersection, half hidden behind a clump of bushes, something flashed. It was sunlight reflecting off the roof of Gritting's silver car.

He must have driven through the gates and down the road a little way, and then, when he thought he couldn't be seen from the house any longer, he had stopped and parked the car. He had never had any intention of leaving. It had been a trick. And he was probably right that minute returning to Brightwood Hall on foot.

Daisy turned and rushed back the way she had come, banging her knee on the window frame in her haste to get through. Gritting had lied to her from the start. He had tried to hurt her. Daisy knew now she hadn't been imagining it, no matter what he'd told her in that fake sad voice of his.

Now he was coming back to finish what he'd started.

She turned this way and that, unable to decide what to do. She had to hide. Was it better to hide here in the bedroom, where she could escape out the window if necessary, or go upstairs where the rooms and corridors were even more crowded than those below, and where it would be harder for Gritting to reach her?

Daisy heard a dry cough from the other side of the room.

"Wondered when you'd notice I was here," Frank said. "You've been running around like a headless emu."

"I need a place to hide!" Daisy panted.

"Headless emus run around for a lot longer than headless chickens," Frank remarked. "Not many people know that."

"I don't need any of your pointless facts! I need a place to hide!"

"Can I be perfectly honest?"

Daisy drew a deep breath. It sounded shuddery. She put her hand on her chest to calm herself.

"That's better," Frank said. She reached into her survival bag and pulled out a paper bag. "You might want to try breathing into this. Sir Clarence finds it useful when he gets the jitters. All sorts of things set him off. Bats, moths, funny-looking trees, running out of toilet paper. I remember one time he—"

"Forget Sir Clarence!" Daisy shouted. "I need to know what to do!"

Frank folded the paper bag and replaced it carefully in the bag. "Seems to me you haven't figured out why this man wants to get rid of you so bad. If you knew that, it might help you decide what to do next. I suggest you have another look at those relics."

"There's no point. I didn't find enough of them to figure anything."

Frank shrugged. "Suit yourself."

"I don't have *time*," Daisy wailed. "He could come back at any minute!"

But Daisy went to the dresser where she'd put the relics. There were four of them: the smashed watch, the letter to her mum, the newspaper clipping, and the card with the kangaroo. She spread them out on the bed.

"I told you. They don't make sense."

"That's because you've got them in the wrong order," Frank informed her, pointing a grubby finger at the bed. "You've got them in the order you found them. You want to order them by age."

"I don't know what you're talking about," Daisy said.

"Arrange them oldest to most recent," Frank explained.

Daisy tried to push aside her panic and think clearly. "I suppose the letter is the oldest," she said. "Gritting sent that to mum when she was only ten. Then there's a big gap, but the kangaroo card comes next. After that, it's the newspaper clipping. The smashed watch is last. It came just a few months ago."

"There you are," Frank said. "Now it's obvious."

"No it's not. I don't see what difference it makes."

"Here's the thing about relics," Frank told her. "They're just bits of something much bigger. What you have to do is fill in the gaps."

"Well, go on, then," Daisy said. "Fill in the gaps!"

Frank folded her arms. "Since I've done all the hard work, I've decided to leave that bit to you."

"You haven't done *anything*," Daisy grumbled. She stared at the relics on the bed. "Okay. Fill in the gaps . . . First there's the letter he wrote."

Gritting had come to Brightwood Hall every summer. After the tragedy with the *Everlasting*, however, he hadn't been allowed to visit anymore. So he had tried asking Daisy's mum, even though she was just a child at the time. Daisy thought it was likely that the letter she'd found wasn't the only one he'd sent. But according to the kangaroo card he'd written some years later, Daisy's mum had ignored all his letters.

Daisy picked up the card and looked at it again.

I hope you have a good life. I certainly will!

"He was angry," Daisy told Frank.

Gritting felt he belonged in Brightwood. He felt he had a right to the place. Hadn't he suggested to Daisy's mum that they turn it into a hotel together? But she'd refused, and so Gritting had left for Australia and gone into partnership with somebody else.

Daisy turned to the newspaper clipping and reread it carefully. It was dated just a year ago. A man who owned hotels in a place called Brisbane had been found dead in a ravine. Daisy didn't know what that had to do with Gritting *or* her mother.

"Do you know where Brisbane is?" she asked Frank.

"Of course I do!" Frank flicked an invisible bug off her shirt and looked away.

"Where is it, then?"

"Do I have to tell you *everything*?"

"You don't know, do you?" Daisy said. "I thought explorers were meant to know things like that."

"I *do* know," Frank insisted. "But I'm certainly not going to tell you now."

"Never mind," Daisy said. "There's an atlas in my bookcase." She looked it up. "It's in Australia."

"Everyone knows that," Frank said.

"Gritting went to Australia!" Daisy said. "What if the man who died in the ravine was his partner? And what if Gritting had something to do with his death?"

Daisy looked at the handwritten words.

Accidents happen!

There was something extremely unpleasant about that exclamation point.

"What if he sent the clipping to Mum as a kind of warning, to show her that it wasn't really an accident at all?"

"That's a lot of 'what-ifs,'" Frank said, clearly still offended by the Brisbane conversation.

"I know," Daisy said. "But look at the next relic, the watch. Gritting stole this from Brightwood Hall when he was a kid. Maybe smashing it was a message. Australia hadn't worked out for him, so he came back and started threatening Mum again."

"I suppose it makes sense," Frank said. "Did your mum seem worried recently?"

"I don't know," Daisy said, trying to remember. "I didn't notice."

"Was she acting differently?"

"Well, she went to the bulk-buy store on Monday," Daisy said. "She *never* goes on a Monday. She always goes on Wednesday."

It was a small detail, although the more Daisy thought about it, the more inexplicable it seemed. Her mum had routines for everything and never varied them without a good reason.

"Don't go anywhere," Daisy told Frank. "I'll be right back."

TWENTY-EIGHT

Daisy went to her mum's bedroom. The last time she had been in here, she had been too busy examining the paintings to pay attention to anything else. Now she took a good long look around.

Among the combs and brushes on her mum's dressing table she saw a Day Box. It was dated the day before her mum had disappeared. But her mum hadn't finished making it. There was only one object inside.

Another envelope. Daisy instantly recognized the handwriting. She reached into the envelope and felt paper and something soft.

It was the little plush kitten that hung from the rear-view mirror of her mum's car. The one that she had treasured but gave to her mum because it was the best thing she had. It was wrapped in a narrow strip of paper that had words written on it in big letters: *Accidents happen!*

Someone had pulled the kitten's head half off.

For a second or two, Daisy stared at the stuffing coming out of its neck, utterly bewildered. She didn't understand what the kitten was doing there. She hadn't noticed it was gone the last time she'd seen the car. But why would she notice something like that? She hadn't been specially looking for it.

Gritting must have taken it. Daisy didn't know when. Perhaps when her mum was out on a recent shopping trip. Were cars easy to break into? Did her mum ever leave hers unlocked? How long had he been following her before he saw his chance? There were too many questions, and Daisy didn't have answers for any of them. Her hands shook as she lifted the piece of paper up to the light.

He had pressed so violently on the dot of the *i* that the pen had gone clear through the paper. It was only a detail, although for some reason it frightened her more than anything else.

Accidents happen!

Gritting had stolen the kitten, and then sent it back damaged as another warning, the worst yet. And the very next day, her mum had disappeared. Gritting must have known she had gone, arriving at Brightwood Hall with a tool to break the padlock on the gates, expecting the place to be empty.

Had he hurt her mum?

Daisy dropped the kitten and backed away, her stomach tight, her legs heavy with dread. She stumbled out of the room and into the Portrait Gallery. Gritting had talked about her mum in the past tense, the way you did when someone was dead. But she couldn't be dead. It wasn't possible.

On the far side of the Portrait Gallery, the General's medals glittered on his chest. Daisy turned away automatically. Then she stopped. Perhaps the shock of finding the kitten had cleared her mind. Or maybe it was simply a matter of being in the right place at the right time. But at that moment, Daisy knew why she had always been frightened of the General and why that fear had grown in the past few days, doubling each time she crossed the Portrait Gallery and caught a glimpse of him from the corner of her eye.

If she looked at the General, looked at him properly, she was afraid she would see some aspect of her mum in his cold, mad face. Something familiar in his features, or the way he held his head. A sign, a mark, a shadow. And then Daisy would know that her mum was crazy too, just as the General had been.

It was a secret fear, so secret that even Daisy herself hadn't been fully aware of it until this moment. Yet now that she was aware, she knew it was completely wrong. Perhaps her mum behaved in ways that people would call crazy. Daisy still didn't know for sure whether that was true. But if it *was* true, it was only sadness that had caused it. Daisy thought of the walls of groceries and the paintings, and Dolly Caroline lying in her little box. It was the sadness of losing nearly everything and everyone you loved.

Her mum wasn't like the General. She didn't have The Crazy. You couldn't catch The Crazy from anyone or get it just by being sad. You had to be born with it.

Daisy walked up to the picture of the General and stared directly at his face. The tips of his long waxed mustache were as sharp as bayonets, and his jacket was the color of fresh blood. But it was his eyes that held her attention.

Daisy knew those eyes. She had seen them just that morning. The same washed-out blue color, the same pupils shrunk to pinholes.

The Crazy ran through the Fitzjohn family. As it ran, it skipped whole generations and then it showed up again.

It wasn't her mum. It was Gritting who had The Crazy. It made you do terrible things. Like sending a thousand men to certain death. Or trying to kill a woman and her daughter just because you wanted what they had.

Daisy knew there was no use talking to Gritting. Or hiding from him, or even trying to fight him. The only thing she could do was run.

TWENTY-NINE

There was no time to pack a bag. Daisy went straight to the window in her bedroom. She slid down the rope by the side of the house, pulling great strands of ivy away from the wall in her haste.

At the bottom, she paused for a moment, her mind racing through her options. Behind her lay the Wilderness. If she took that route, it would take her a long time to make her way through the dense undergrowth. Another possibility was to climb the perimeter wall on either side of the grounds. But then she would be far from the road, and if Gritting saw her, he might catch her on the other side. Her best option was to make for the main gates.

Someone in a passing car might see her, and even if there were no cars, she could follow the road to wherever it led.

Except she didn't know where it led. For a split second, Daisy's fear of the outside world was almost as great as her fear of Gritting himself. She shook her head. The road led to people, she told herself. It led to *help*.

She ran across the front of the house, keeping to the cover of bushes wherever she could. When she got to the topiary, she made a dash for the area of trees just beyond and crouched down, panting, her eyes on the long sweep of meadow that lay between her and the gates.

It was empty. The air was still, and she could hear the murmur of insects. Far off, a blackbird called its familiar, reassuring song.

Daisy took a deep breath and plunged into the meadow, running bent double through the long grasses, gnats rising in clouds above her head.

It was a long way to the gates. She reached a cedar tree and rested for a moment or two in its green shadow, her heart pounding. The gates were a hundred yards away. She could cover the distance in a little more than thirty seconds if she sprinted.

Daisy took off in a headlong dash towards the Lookout Tree. She had climbed it a hundred times and knew its many perches as well as she knew the great staircase of Brightwood Hall itself.

From its long, overhanging branches, she could look over the perimeter wall, and if Gritting was nowhere to be seen, she could drop down to the grassy edge of the road.

She reached the tree and started pulling herself up, her toes finding cracks in the bark, her arms reaching for familiar handholds. She was crawling on her belly along one of the lower branches, when a noise made her look down.

Gritting was standing just below, staring straight up at her.

The shock sent Daisy slipping sideways, her hands grasping at empty air. She fell at his feet, all the breath knocked out of her, and he grabbed her before she had a chance to move.

"Making a run for it?" He lifted her up by her arm as if she weighed no more than a bundle of rags.

Daisy was too busy struggling to reply. But it was no use.

"Where's my mum?" she cried. "What have you done to her?"

"We're not going to talk about that," Gritting said. "I was going to wait until it got dark and then surprise you. But I underestimated you from the start. You're far more sneaky than I thought."

"*You're* the sneaky one!" Daisy shouted. "You're a sneak and a liar!"

"I think you and I need to take a little walk," Gritting said, ignoring her outburst. "Turn around, that's right."

He took hold of the collar of her shirt, and they went up the driveway towards the house. Whenever she slowed or hesitated, he gave her a little shove.

"I'm glad you're not trying to run," Gritting said. "It would be a pity if I had to hurt you. It would be hard to make it look like an accident."

Daisy remembered her knife, still stuck in the waistband of her trousers. Gritting hadn't seen it because her shirt covered it.

"I don't understand," she said, trying to distract him.

"I like accidents," Gritting said. "It was the yacht blowing up that first sparked my interest."

"The *Everlasting*?"

"That's the one. I didn't have anything to do with the accident, although you could say it inspired me. Afterwards, I realized that once the old lady, your great-grandmother, died, your mother and I would be the only members of the Fitzjohn family left. We'd be the last heirs to Brightwood. My own mother didn't count. She was never in the best of health. That was why I was sent here every summer."

How casually he talked about people dying.

"I saw how convenient accidents could be," Gritting continued. "Ever since then, they've been a specialty of mine."

They were at the front of the house now. From the corner of her eye, Daisy could see the topiary with True's body lying at its center. Sweat ran down her neck and trickled under her arms. Gritting gave her another shove. She turned down the path towards the walled gardens.

"Please just tell me what's happened to my mum," Daisy begged.

"Let's just say she's not acting crazy anymore," Gritting said.

You're the one with The Crazy! Daisy thought.

"It didn't have to come to this," Gritting said. "I was polite. I was *reasonable*. I sent your mother letter after letter, telling her she had to share this place with me. That's all I asked for! To share it, to make it into something. There's room for a hotel *and* a golf course. Cut down the trees and drain the lake, and you've got land for twenty or more luxury homes."

Daisy remembered how he had spent a whole day measuring everything with his little wheel and stick.

"Your mother wouldn't see sense," Gritting said. "Eventually I gave up and went abroad."

"To Australia," Daisy said. "I found the card you sent."

"You *have* been a good little detective!" Gritting said, shoving her again.

"That partner of yours. It wasn't an accident, was it?"

"He was about to accuse me of stealing money from our company," Gritting said. "He fell down a cliff instead."

"Don't you have feelings?" Daisy burst out. "Don't you care about *anything*?"

He didn't reply. They had passed the glasshouse, and now they stood on the edge of the Wilderness. The path that led through the trees was dark and narrow. Daisy looked quickly from left to right.

"Don't get any ideas," Gritting said. His grip tightened on her collar. "Remember, I know this place almost as well as you do."

The branches of the trees were laced together, forming a tunnel over the path. Brambles tore at Daisy's trousers. The path wound into a nettle bush and then disappeared. Gritting pushed her onwards, through the stinging leaves.

In the distance, Daisy heard the sound of the old stable chain, clanking steadily as if to summon her. She shrank back.

"I don't like it here," she said. "I don't want to go."

But they were already at the stables. Ramshackle buildings surrounded a yard. Doors hung from their frames and vines tugged at the walls. Through the empty windows, Daisy glimpsed the dark shapes of long-forgotten things, made strange by rot and creeping weeds.

Gritting nudged her to the center of the yard. He kicked at a wooden board that lay on the ground, shifting it sideways to reveal the black mouth of a well. Daisy drew back in surprise and fear. She never went to the stables and hadn't known there was a well there.

"They used it to water the horses in the old days," Gritting said. "I used to come here when I was a kid, before they covered it up. It was one of my favorite spots."

He paused. "You asked me whether I cared about anything. The only thing I care about is Brightwood Hall. It's the only place I've ever belonged. The Fitzjohns couldn't see it, of course. They made a great pretense of being kind, but they never liked me. I didn't fit in with their stupid parties and gardening and tennis. I didn't care. It didn't matter. It still doesn't matter. Do you know why?"

Daisy shook her head. Somewhere deep in the other side of the Wilderness, a peacock gave a shrill scream.

"Because accidents happen," Gritting said, and pushed her into the well.

THIRTY

Daisy fell, too shocked to scream, her body scraping against the wall of the well. She landed on a thick layer of leaves, the smell of mold and damp stone thick in her nostrils.

She was stunned. It was almost completely dark, but when she turned her head, she could see a blue circle of sky about fifteen feet above. The outline of Gritting's head and shoulders appeared at the edge of the circle; he was looking down. But Daisy was in shadow and he couldn't see her. After a long moment, he disappeared.

Daisy shifted and felt a searing pain down her right leg. She struggled to her knees, feeling her way in the darkness. The well was narrow; she could easily touch both sides when she stretched out her arms. But as she did so, the leaves shifted beneath her, and she heard the sound of cracking wood from somewhere deep below.

She stopped short. She hadn't landed at the bottom of the well. Instead she'd fallen onto a layer of leaves and branches that blocked it partway down. The cracking wood must have been the sound of those branches starting to give way under her weight.

Daisy groped along the wall, frantically searching for hand-holds. The stone was perfectly smooth. Her leg burned and she shifted, trying to get comfortable. The crack of wood came again, louder and more ominous.

There was nothing she could do but stay as still as possible.

Her breath came fast, faster even than her heartbeat, the air squeezed to a whimper as it reached her throat. No solitary traveler in the desert or astronaut drifting in endless space had ever felt more helpless or alone. She closed her eyes and clenched her fists, willing Frank to appear. Even a girl who wasn't there would be better than nobody at all.

But Frank came only when it suited her, and when Daisy opened her eyes, she saw nothing except darkness.

She started to cry, too terrified to brush the tears away in case even this tiny movement dislodged her perch among the leaves.

"What are you blubbing about *this* time?"

The voice came from above. Daisy looked up. Frank was sitting on the edge of the well with her legs dangling down. Silhouetted against the sky, her black-and-white had faded to gray. In places she was almost transparent. Daisy could look right through her body and see the dim shapes of drifting clouds.

"Isn't it obvious?" Daisy said, still crying.

"You've gotten yourself into a tight spot," Frank said.

"I didn't get myself in here!" Daisy protested. "I was pushed!"

Frank's outline seemed to flicker against the sky.

"Don't go!" Daisy cried. "Tell me how to get out of this . . . What would you call it? A cave? Another tomb?"

Frank shook her head in a pitying way. "It's a well," she said. "Anyone can see that."

For a split second, Daisy felt so irritated that she forgot to be afraid. "I do *know* that," she muttered.

"Why did you call it a cave, then? It doesn't look anything like a cave."

Daisy's leg hurt worse than ever. She reached down cautiously and felt her trousers. They were wet and sticky.

"I'm bleeding."

"That?" Frank snorted slightly. "It's barely a scratch."

"How do you know?"

"You've got to pull yourself together," Frank said.

"I can't move!"

"Reminds me of when Sir Clarence wandered into some quicksand," Frank remarked. "The more he thrashed about, the deeper he sank. Poor Sir Clarence," she added. "How he squealed!"

"Did you pull him out?"

"Certainly not!" Frank said. "I didn't go anywhere near him. He'd have dragged me in too. I told him that in a quicksand situation, you've got to widen the space between your legs and then bring them up to the surface until you're horizontal."

Daisy stared at her blankly.

"Not many people know that," Frank said.

"I don't know what that's got to do with me," Daisy said. "I'm not stuck in quicksand."

"You can bring your legs up, can't you?"

Daisy considered the suggestion. If she braced her feet against one side of the well and her arms against the opposite side, she might be able to move upwards in much the same way she had traveled through the blocked corridor after discovering her mum's old bedroom.

But it was a long way to the top. Daisy doubted she could make it even if her leg hadn't been hurt.

"If I fall," she said, "I'll probably crash right through this layer of leaves. I'll fall to the bottom of the well."

"Probably," Frank agreed.

"You don't have to sound so casual about it!"

"Can I be perfectly honest?"

"No!" Daisy shouted. "No, you can't! I'm not doing it. It's too risky."

Frank swung her legs over the side of the well. "I'll be off, then. It's been nice knowing you."

"Where are you going?"

"I've got places to get to," Frank said. She glanced briefly down at Daisy.

"Hey!" Daisy yelled.

But Frank had disappeared.

"Hey!" Daisy called again. "Is that it? Is that all the help I get?"

For a moment, she felt so angry that she didn't have room to feel scared. Without thinking about it, she jumped. She braced her feet and arms against the sides of the well and began furiously shifting herself upwards, inch by inch.

THIRTY-ONE

Daisy had no idea how long she had climbed. The instant she braced herself against the sides of the well, her leg began to hurt twice as much as it had before. By the time she had moved up a few feet, it felt as though she had a knife stuck there. She heard herself groaning as she sweated her way up, the skin on her shoulders rubbing raw against the stone.

Well before Daisy was halfway to the top, most of the feeling had gone from her arms. She kept her gaze fixed on the lip of the well and the circle of sky, although it seemed she was getting no nearer—and after a while, she lost the hope that she would ever get out.

Now Daisy climbed simply out of fear. If she slipped, she would fall through the leaves and branches, down to the very dark, where nobody could reach her and there was no hope of escape.

She would never get to the top. She would climb forever, halfway between earth and sky. Her lungs hurt and a tremor started up in her legs, the sign of muscles pushed to the limit of their strength. Yet she couldn't stop to rest. Braced as she was against the walls, even staying still would use up what little energy she had left. She closed her eyes and kept going.

At last, Daisy sensed fresh air. The top of the well was suddenly within reach. A few more inches and she was there, her feet scrabbling against the upper stones, her shoulders heaving over the edge.

She lay in a heap by the side of the well for a long time, too weak to move. Then she got to her feet and began to head back through the Wilderness, aiming for the place where the undergrowth gave way to lawn.

Her leg had grown numb, and although the pain had lessened, Daisy couldn't rest her full weight on it. She limped along as best she could. Thorns tore at her trousers and she hesitated, unsure of the way, before stumbling on again, her throat aching with thirst, her hands smeared with dirt and tears.

It was a relief when the trees began to thin, and she pushed through the last bushes to find herself on the edge of the lawn, with the topiary on her right and the meadow stretching ahead of her.

If she hurried, she could be at the main gates in a few minutes. She was just about to set off at a limping run when she instead stopped abruptly.

Gritting was in front of her, barely fifty feet away.

They saw each other at exactly the same moment.

Without wasting a second, he rushed towards her, plunging heavily through the long grass.

At any other time, Daisy would have been able to dodge him and still reach the main gates. He was too large to be nimble on his feet. Now, with her injured leg, she couldn't risk it. Instead she turned and fled in the other direction, towards the house.

She had only a small lead, and by the sound of Gritting's thundering feet behind her, it was getting smaller by the second. She staggered over the gravel and nearly fell, but managed to regain her balance and get to the front door. There was no time to shut it. She raced through the Marble Hall, plunged into one of the passageways, and then, with great difficulty, scrambled up a shelving unit. She scuttled as fast as she could across the tops of the shelves until she reached the pile of Day Boxes she had built the night before.

Daisy lay flat on her stomach behind the boxes, her chest heaving.

Gritting didn't shout or call her name, although Daisy knew he was somewhere below, perhaps still trying to figure out how to enter the maze. Then she heard his steps coming at a rapid trot down the first cleared passageway. He turned the corner, and the steps came louder as he passed her hiding place.

Daisy rose to her knees, moving in perfect silence. Slowly she peered around the boxes. Gritting was below her and to the left, in the central clearing. As she watched, he turned his head and looked around him, then stepped forward so carefully that his feet made no noise.

His white shirt was a perfect target, even from this distance and this angle. Daisy reached for her knife. She could hit him—she knew she could.

Her grip tightened on the knife. Then she paused.

What was it True had said?

In the end, the only thing that matters is to keep your Shape.

Daisy exhaled slowly. She wasn't a killer. The Crazy had skipped clean over her.

I have to keep my Shape, she thought.

She lowered her arm, abandoning the knife, and glanced at the pile of boxes. There was still the temple trap. In a few seconds, Gritting would realize that there were no more cleared passageways and he was at a dead end. Then he would retrace his steps and her only chance would be gone. There was no time to waste and no point in being quiet any longer. She jumped to her feet and threw her shoulder against the pile.

It gave way at once, and Daisy almost lost her balance for a moment. She teetered back, half blinded by flying dust as the boxes tumbled to the ground, blocking the narrow passageway. The noise was far louder than she had expected: a whole orchestra of crashes and thuds, of shattering glass and bursting cardboard and the sharp, machine-gun patter as a thousand objects were hurled in all directions.

And then, before Daisy had time to gather her wits, she heard another, quite different sound: a long, dry, creaking groan that seemed to reach her bones and make them shudder.

A dark crack was running across the broad white ceiling of the Marble Hall. The avalanche of falling boxes must have found a weakness in the ancient walls, shifting the structure of the house itself.

It took only a heartbeat for Daisy to see that the crack was spreading, running with inexorable speed towards the chandelier. It was no bigger than a thread, although it was growing wider and pieces of ceiling plaster were already breaking away.

Daisy threw up her arms to shield herself, but it was too late. A chunk of plaster the size of her fist struck the side of her head, and she lost her footing on the narrow perch. She would have fallen straight to the ground except that as she fell, she grabbed at the top of the shelving unit and her fingers caught on a tiny ridge right on the edge.

She hung from her arms, more than fifteen feet above the ground.

Daisy instantly realized just how unlucky she had been. If she had fallen on the far side of the blocked passageway, she might have hurt herself dropping to the ground, but she still would have had a chance of getting out of the house while Gritting struggled to clear boxes out of his way.

Instead she was on the other side.

She turned her head. Gritting hadn't moved from the clearing. He stood still, his face oddly calm as he stared up at her.

"Now what are you going to do?" he said.

Daisy tried to swing her lower body up to reach a nearby shelf, but her injured leg was as stiff and as heavy as wood.

"It seems to me that I have two options," Gritting said in a thoughtful voice. "I can use some of those boxes to climb up and pull you down. Or I can just wait here until you fall all by yourself."

Daisy didn't have the strength to reply. Her arms, weakened by her long climb out of the well, felt as if they were being pulled slowly but surely out of their sockets.

"I think I'll wait," Gritting announced. He folded his arms across his chest and gazed at her with an interested expression. "Question is, what will *you* do? Will you give up at once, or will you hang there for as long as you possibly can, even though you know it's useless?"

Daisy wondered briefly whether she could inch along the top of the shelving unit until she was safely on the other side of the blocked passageway. Yet she knew it was impossible. Her fingers were already cramped. If she moved them even slightly, she would fall.

But she would fall anyway, sooner or later. Perhaps falling would be better than this pain.

"My partner in Australia hung on for over two minutes," Gritting said. "I timed him. I don't think you'll last nearly that long."

Daisy gritted her teeth. She wondered whether she could hold on for even ten seconds more. Ten seconds suddenly seemed an impossible stretch of time. The noise of the plaster cracking above her had stopped, and apart from her own dry, desperate breaths, silence filled the Marble Hall.

Then, as she hung there, her will almost exhausted and her

strength quite gone, she heard a familiar sound, faint at first but growing louder as it grew nearer. It was the tinkling rattle of a chain, swaying gently from side to side.

With a huge effort that almost dislodged her grip on the top of the shelving unit, Daisy twisted her head and looked up.

THIRTY-TWO

Among all the things that had been stored away in Brightwood Hall, Daisy had once found a collection of tiny books, each no larger than two inches wide. They had pictures inside. When she held one in her left hand and flipped through it very fast with her right, the pictures in the book all joined together in a single movement. It was only when she flipped through a book slowly that she saw that each of the pictures was actually separate from the others.

It was exactly the same as she looked up now. As if every tiny fraction of a second were a separate picture being slowly flipped. Daisy saw Tar running along the chain towards the chandelier.

Then she saw him pause, struggling for balance as the chain swung wide.

The Marble Hall had stood strong for over two hundred and fifty years. Now Daisy watched the crack in the ceiling widen to a chasm as Tar added his weight to the chandelier.

Gritting was frozen below, his face turned up in astonishment. A great wrenching noise filled the air like something huge being pulled up by the roots, and the chandelier swayed and rang as fragments of masonry struck its shivering glass.

Then, with a groan so deep and sorrowful that it shook the house, the wheel and pulley ripped from the ceiling and the chain snaked free.

For a split second, Daisy saw Gritting, his eyes wide, his body trying to pivot away. Then the chandelier fell with all the weight of its ten thousand crystal tears, and Gritting disappeared.

Daisy must have fallen at the same time, although she had no sense of it. She lay curled on the floor, her arms covering her head. The enormous, thudding crunch of the chandelier hitting the ground was followed by the silvery tinkle of hundreds of pieces of glass flying and shattering in all directions.

But it wasn't the end. The end came with a splitting of wood and a violent rumbling that made Daisy scream. She flung herself back, scrambling over boxes and broken china. The floor had collapsed under the weight of glass and twisted metal. She heard a shuddering crash as the chandelier burst through hidden layers of wood and brick and landed on the floor of the basement far below.

Daisy gaped at the huge hole where the central clearing had once been, hardly daring to move. Gritting was nowhere to be seen. He must have fallen with the chandelier. Daisy knew he was surely dead.

An accident had killed him. The Hunter would have said there was poetic justice in that fact. But Daisy couldn't feel any satisfaction. Only a deep sickness in her stomach.

The passageway behind her was blocked with boxes. Moving with great caution and taking care to keep as far away from the hole in the floor as possible, Daisy inched around the closest shelving unit and slipped into the next passageway. She turned sideways, navigating through the stacked shelves like a crab, and after a few moments, she emerged safely at the other end.

Walking slowly now, her mind dazed, Daisy went up the great staircase to her room. There was nothing left to do except pack her bag.

THIRTY-THREE

Daisy put what she needed into her bag and turned to leave. Out in the Portrait Gallery, she took a last look at Little Charles.

"You can't go!" His voice was a pleading whisper. "You said you'd give me more room. I want to see my nanny."

It hardly mattered now if she made a mess with the books.

"I love my nanny," Little Charles said. "She's the only one I love."

Little Charles's painting was not particularly large. In a few moments, Daisy had cleared the books that had been hiding it. There he stood with his hoop and his dog, Minette. A man and a woman were behind him in the room. The man wore tight trousers and a jacket with a lot of buttons. The woman was dressed in a shining white gown that covered her feet. They both had long noses and a proud, haughty look.

"Is that your mum and dad?"

Little Charles nodded, his face woebegone. "They're very grand. I have to call them 'Sir' and 'Madam.' It's only Nanny who hugs me."

Daisy examined the painting carefully. She could see no other figure in the room.

"She's not there, is she?" Little Charles said. "I hoped and hoped she would be, but she's just a commoner and commoners aren't good enough to be painted."

"You're a terrible snob, Little Charles," Daisy said.

"I know," he said with great sadness. "All the best people are." His eyes glistened.

"Don't cry, Little Charles."

"I can't help it," he said. "I miss her so."

"I know where your nanny is," Daisy said.

"You do?"

She nodded.

"Where is she?"

"You can't see it," Daisy told him, "but there's a door painted in the back of the room you're standing in."

She leaned forward, gazing at the little scene. "The door is closed. But your nanny is right behind it. She's got her hand raised to knock."

"Does she have bread and honey for me?"

"Yes," Daisy said. "Three whole slices. And after you've eaten, she's going to take you out to play. You'll be able to run with your hoop, Little Charles."

He gazed at her, his eyes wide. "Promise?"

"Promise," Daisy said. She touched his painted face with the tip of her finger. "Good-bye, Little Charles."

As she walked away, Daisy thought she heard the click of a door and the murmur of voices behind her. Then—quite clear and distinct—a cry of joy.

Daisy didn't turn to see. She adjusted her bag on her shoulder and went down the great staircase without looking back.

She paused halfway. A dark shape was crouched on the bottom stair.

"Tar!" Daisy cried, running down. She reached for the rat and picked him up carefully. "I thought you must be dead."

"I told you rats have ten lives," Tar said, squirming in her hands.

"You must have used nine of them when that chain came down."

"I used four," Tar corrected her, a little crossly. "It's important to keep count."

"I'm going," Daisy said. "But I can't leave you behind. Who would feed you?"

He squirmed even harder, his eyes bulging.

"You're frightened," she said. "I know you are. There's nothing to worry about, Tar. We'll go out of the house and walk down the driveway, and when we get to the gates, we'll just keep on walking."

Daisy drew a deep breath.

"You'll see. It's going to be all right."

"What are you talking about?" Tar said peevishly. "I'm always all right. I've been to the outside world zillions of times. It's just the same as here, only there's more of it."

"Are you sure?"

"Positive."

Daisy put him in her pocket and stood up. "Okay," she said. "I'm ready."

Outside on the lawn, Frank was waiting for her. She was fainter than before, no more than a gray shadow above the grass.

"I told you the temple trap would work," she said.

"It didn't work the way you thought," Daisy said, although she didn't feel like arguing.

"He's dead, isn't he?"

Daisy nodded.

"Well, then."

Frank flickered and seemed to lose substance, her figure nothing but a wisp in the dusk. A white moth flew up from the grass and fluttered clean through her. Daisy felt a great sadness, too mysterious for tears.

"Please don't vanish," she whispered. "Come with me."

"I'm not on that expedition," Frank said. "You won't need me."

"Don't you *want* to come?" Daisy said. "Think of all the new places you'll see."

Frank didn't answer. But her face came into sharp focus for a moment, and the look of longing in her eyes was enough to break Daisy's heart.

"It's not an option," Frank said. "There's no use blubbing about it."

"*Why* isn't it an option?"

"You know why."

Daisy hesitated. Then she nodded. Frank could explore the jungles and deserts and endless snowcapped mountains of the made-up world. But not the real one.

The real world was a place she could never travel to.

"But *you* can," Frank said. She was so faint now that Daisy had to stare hard to make out her shape. Her voice was barely louder than the breeze in the grass.

"Go for me . . . "

"I will," Daisy said. "You'll see—I will. I promise."

She closed her eyes and turned away. If she stayed any longer, she would start to cry and that would be letting Frank down.

She walked slowly along the driveway, keeping her eyes fixed on the main gates. She didn't want to look back and see nothing except grass and trees and the terrible empty space where Frank had been.

THIRTY-FOUR

Daisy stood at the main gates with the two stone lions, Royal and Regal, on either side. As she passed between them, she expected them to try to stop her with their usual tears and warnings. But they were completely silent.

A few more steps, and then Daisy was outside.

She stopped, listening for voices calling for her return, or the creak of the house itself reaching to pull her back. No sound came. Brightwood Hall was the only place where Daisy had ever existed. Perhaps it was the only place where she *could* exist, and she would simply vanish now that the gates were behind her.

But she was still there, still visible. And the sky was the same, and the air. She wrapped her arms around her body. She could feel her heart and the unfamiliar texture of the road beneath her feet. In the daze of leaving, she had forgotten to put on her shoes.

Daisy thought that if she went back to fetch them, she wouldn't find the courage to leave for a second time. She looked left and right, and set off slowly in the direction where she knew the village lay, walking on the grass by the side of the road.

The sun had dipped into the long dusk of summer, and the road was clear ahead. Daisy kept her head down, willing herself to keep walking without looking back.

But how could she *not* look back? She could still sense the house behind her, with all its beloved corners, its stately trees and secret pathways, its mornings and its nights. Down dusty corridors, ten thousand memories lay stored. All dreams were there, all stories too.

Daisy turned her head for one last look.

She had never seen Brightwood Hall from outside the grounds. It looked different, oddly distant. The house a little smaller, the wall a fraction lower. This was the view that people passing on the road must have, she thought. This was the Brightwood they saw. And now, Daisy saw it too. The realization brought a rush of grief, as if she had lost a part of herself and would never get it back, no matter how long she lived.

She stroked the outside of her pocket, feeling Tar's warm shape.

"Don't be sad, Tar," she whispered. "It's all right . . ."

She carried on down the road, reassured a little by the sight of familiar trees and bushes. Brightwood Hall was full of the same sort of plants. Then the trees thinned out, and there were fields on either side, fenced by wire and slender wooden posts.

The fields stretched towards a far horizon. Daisy couldn't see where they ended. She had always known what lay around every corner, her world mapped to the last box of groceries, the smallest clearing in the grass. Now there was no telling what lay beyond the fields, or behind the curving road. Her breath quickened with fear.

"It's just fields," she told Tar. "It's just a bend in the road."

He wriggled, and she pinched her pocket tight between her fingers.

"It's like you said it was," Daisy said. "The outside world is just the same, except there's more of it."

After it curved, the road ran up a hill and then dipped down in a long straight line, with little except low hedges and the occasional tree on either side. Daisy trudged on. She had been walking for twenty minutes without a single car passing. Then three came, one after the other.

The first one was blue, and it drove by so fast that she almost fell backwards with the surprise of it. The second car was also blue, and it slowed down a little as it went by, as if it were thinking of stopping but decided against it at the last moment.

The third car was white, and it stopped on the road right next to her.

Daisy stopped too, although she didn't look at the car. She kept her gaze fixed on the grassy edge of the road. She heard the car window being rolled down.

"Do you need a ride?" It was a woman's voice.

Daisy was too frightened to answer.

"Where are you going?"

Daisy risked a quick look at the driver of the car. She saw a dark-haired woman staring back at her, a worried expression in her eyes. The woman's gaze moved down to Daisy's bare feet and then back up to her face.

"Where's your mother, sweetheart?"

The question was so astonishing that Daisy's heart seemed to stop beating for a second or two. How did the woman know Daisy's mum was missing? How could she tell she was looking for her?

"I don't know," Daisy said, her voice breaking a little.

"You're as white as a sheet," the woman said, "Are you all right?"

She sounded so kind that tears rose in Daisy's eyes.

"There's a m-man in my house!" Daisy burst out before she could stop herself. "He's dead. He's an uncle or a cousin. I didn't, I didn't . . . "

The woman got out of the car and closed the door behind her. She leaned down, searching Daisy's face with her eyes.

"It's okay, sweetheart," she said. "What's your name?"

"Daisy. Daisy Fitzjohn."

The woman paused, and for a terrible moment, Daisy thought she was about to say that there was no such person, just as Gritting had done. But the woman only smiled.

"How old are you, Daisy?"

"Eleven."

"It's going to be okay," the woman said, straightening up. "Although you can't be out all by yourself. It's at least ten miles to the village. Hop in the car, and we'll get this all sorted out in no time."

Daisy hesitated. She felt the woman's hand, gentle on her back.

"It's going to be okay," the woman repeated. "I promise."

The car door opened, and then Daisy was inside. She sat in the front seat, next to the woman, every muscle in her body clenched. The fields ran by in a green blur.

"The man in your house," the woman ventured, her eyes fixed on the road ahead. "The one you said was . . . dead. Where do you live, sweetheart?"

"In Brightwood Hall," Daisy said. She tried to talk slowly, to explain, but the words came out in a gulping rush. "It's just me and my mum, only she didn't come home and he came instead and I asked him to go, but . . . but he wouldn't and he killed the rabbits and the chandelier fell down on him."

Daisy knew she hadn't made any sense, but the woman only nodded.

"I think the best thing to do," she said, "is call ahead and let the police know we're coming."

THIRTY-FIVE

It took nearly half an hour to drive to the village, and Daisy had time to relax a fraction and even to look out of the window. But the car was driving so fast and the things she saw were so odd that she didn't have much time to make sense of them. There were poles, all the same height, with wire strung between them like washing lines, even though the wire was far too high to hang clothes from it. Cows stood in a field, mysteriously still.

In the middle of nowhere, a sign said STOP. Yet there was no sign telling you when you could start again.

After a while, the fields disappeared and Daisy saw tiny houses, with even tinier gardens in the front, and a building with a tower that rose to a sharp spike. It was a church. The same church whose spire she had seen a thousand times from her perch in the Lookout Tree at Brightwood Hall.

The car slowed and turned into a wide space with a lot of other cars.

"This is the police station," the woman told Daisy. "They'll look after you here."

Daisy got a confused impression of a wide entrance with lights overhead. Then the woman who had been driving the car vanished, and another woman wearing a uniform appeared and took Daisy by the hand.

Daisy didn't want to hold hands, but she was too scared to pull away. The policewoman's shoes made a loud clacking noise on the shiny floor. They entered a room with a sofa and chairs and a low table in the center. It was the emptiest room Daisy had ever seen.

"Let me take your bag," the policewoman said, reaching for it. Daisy jerked away.

"That's all right, you can keep it. You're Daisy, aren't you? My name is Mrs. Gardner."

She guided Daisy to the sofa and fetched a blanket and wrapped it around Daisy's shoulders. Daisy hadn't felt cold, but under the blanket, she began to shake. She sat as still as possible, hugging her bag tight to her chest.

"Would you like something to drink?"

Daisy shook her head.

"Do you want to tell me what happened?" Mrs. Gardner's voice was calm, although Daisy didn't dare to raise her head. Instead she kept her gaze fixed on the buttons on Mrs. Gardner's shirt.

"That's okay," Mrs. Gardner said. "You can take your time."

There were six buttons. They were white and the top one was undone. Under the blanket, Daisy's shaking grew worse.

"Take your time," Mrs. Gardner repeated. "Are you hungry? Would you like something to eat? A sandwich maybe?"

Daisy shook her head again.

At the mention of sandwiches, Tar woke up and squirmed against her leg. She pinched her pocket closed but she could feel him wriggling frantically, searching for a way out.

"Are you all right?" Mrs. Gardner asked. "You look uncomfortable."

Daisy pinched her pocket tighter. It was no use. Even though he was small, Tar was strong and he was used to getting out of tight corners. She felt his head pushing against her fingers, and a second later he had escaped into her lap. Daisy's eyes shot to Mrs. Gardner's face. She had expected her to cry out in surprise.

But Mrs. Gardner didn't seem at all worried by Tar's appearance. She leaned forward for a better look.

"Is that your pet?" she asked. "What a lovely color he is!"

Daisy stroked Tar's back with trembling fingers.

"What's his name?"

"Tar."

"I can tell you're a clever girl, Daisy," Mrs. Gardner said. "That's *rat* spelled backwards, isn't it?"

Daisy nodded. Perhaps Mrs. Gardner was a friend after all.

"My mum went out in the car nearly a week ago," she said, lifting her head. "I waited and waited, only she didn't come back."

Slowly at first, and then with growing confidence, Daisy described the events of the past six days. It took a long time and all the way through, Mrs. Gardner kept her eyes on Daisy's face. Every so often she nodded and once or twice she pressed her lips together as though she was holding back words, but she didn't interrupt.

Daisy was just coming to the end, when there was a knock at the door. A man in a dark blue uniform came in. When he saw Tar, his eyes widened and he made a coughing noise. Mrs. Gardner frowned at him.

"Could I have a word?" he said.

They were out of the room for nearly five minutes. Daisy waited, rather regretting now that she had refused the sandwich. Tar regretted it too. He stared at her with an outraged look on his face.

"I'm sorry," she whispered. "I'll get you something as soon as I can."

But when Mrs. Gardner came back into the room, Daisy could see by her face that she was thinking about something quite different from sandwiches.

She sat down on the sofa next to Daisy. "I have news," she said. "It's about your mother."

Daisy couldn't speak. Mrs. Gardner took her hand, and this time Daisy didn't want to pull away.

"She's called Caroline, isn't she? Caroline Fitzjohn."

Daisy nodded.

Mrs. Gardner hesitated. Her hand tightened. Or perhaps it was Daisy herself who was squeezing it, terrified of what she might hear next.

"She was in a car accident," Mrs. Gardner said. "She came off the road. It was a hit-and-run. Do you know what that is?"

Daisy shook her head.

"It's when the person responsible leaves the scene of an accident without identifying himself or herself. We found paint marks on your mother's car, suggesting that whoever hit her was driving a silver-colored vehicle."

Gritting, Daisy thought. She had seen the long scrape down the right-hand side of his car. He had forced her mum off the road and made it look like an accident.

"Is she dead?" Daisy said, surprised at how steady her voice sounded. Mrs. Gardner shook her head. "No, Daisy, she's not dead. But she's in the hospital. She's been badly hurt. She's still unconscious."

"I want to see her," Daisy said.

"It's very late. We'll get you there first thing in the morning."

"No," Daisy said. She stood up, shaking off the blanket. "I want to see her *now*."

Mrs. Gardner didn't say anything for a moment. Then she nodded. "Okay," she said. "I understand."

Daisy was hardly aware of anything at all on the ride to the hospital. The journey might have taken five minutes, or an hour. There might have been two people in the car with her, or maybe three. It was dark outside, and she could see nothing except the glare and dazzle of passing vehicles.

The car went by a long row of overhead lights that turned Daisy's hands a sickly yellow color. She wanted to close her eyes, but she couldn't. Then the dark swallowed up the car again, and they carried on for what might have been a hundred miles, or only ten.

Daisy held her bag tight on her lap. She had left Tar behind at the police station. Mrs. Gardner had said she would look after him until Daisy returned. She wished he were with her now, despite all his wriggling and his nagging for food.

They pulled up under a big awning, lit by more of the sickly yellow light. Then they were out of the car, walking through a huge glass door into a building that looked like the Marble Hall, only far bigger and with nowhere to hide. Daisy shrank back at the sight of so many people.

Hands guided her forward. She went up a staircase and down a long, shining corridor with double doors that opened silently without needing to be touched. Daisy felt exhaustion rising. Faces blurred around her. Now she was in a room and people were talking, although she didn't understand what they were saying.

"We operated to relieve the pressure," a man said. His face was so close that Daisy could see her reflection in his glasses. "We're keeping her stable."

Daisy felt herself sway, and the room tilted a fraction.

That makes no sense, she thought. *You can't keep her there. My mum's not a horse!*

". . . not responding, I'm afraid," the man was saying. "Everything possible is being done . . . "

Two young women wearing strange green overalls led Daisy to a door with the shade pulled down.

"Let me take your bag," one of them said.

"No," Daisy whispered. *"No."*

"Just a few minutes. You understand?" the woman said.

"Oh, let her stay," the other one murmured in a soft voice. "What harm can it possibly do now?"

They opened the door. Daisy saw a dimly lit room. Her mum lay on a bed, almost completely surrounded by machines and devices. There were tubes coming out of her arms. Her eyes were closed. Her hair had been cut close to her scalp, and one side of her head was covered with a white bandage.

"Oh, Mum," Daisy said. "You have short hair now, just like me."

She climbed onto the bed and lay down. Her mum didn't speak or even stir as Daisy nestled against her. Daisy reached for her mum's hand and placed it against her own cheek.

"I found you," Daisy said.

A second later, she was fast asleep.

DAY SEVEN

THIRTY-SIX

The early morning light came through the window blinds in thin stripes. The strangeness of it woke Daisy up. Her mum's hand lay unmoving on the blanket, just in front of her eyes. Daisy stared at it uncomprehendingly for a moment. Then she sat up.

"Mum?"

Her mother looked as if she were simply asleep. Daisy leaned forward and touched her face.

"Mum?"

Her mother's skin was warm, but she didn't move or open her eyes.

"It's me!" Daisy cried. "It's Daisy!"

She could hear a faint humming sound coming from all around. It was the noise of the hospital waking up. Panic seized her.

"Mum!"

She grabbed her mum's hand and squeezed it hard. It was thinner than she remembered, the fingers delicate, with faint marks of paint still under the nails.

"You have to wake up," Daisy said. "You *have* to!"

A man and a woman came into the room. They were wearing the same pale green overalls as the women the night before.

"Who are you?" Daisy said, confused.

"We're nurses," one of them said, giving her an odd look.

"It's time to go," the other said. "You'll be wanting some breakfast."

Daisy shook her head.

"You can come back later," the first nurse said. "You can't stay here now. The doctor needs to make his rounds."

Daisy held on tight to her mother's hand. "I can't leave," she said. "I have to wake up my mum."

The first nurse made a face, her mouth turned down. "I know you feel that way, honey, but . . . "

"We're doing everything we can for her," the other added.

"You don't understand," Daisy said, her voice rising.

The first nurse had her hand on Daisy's shoulder and was steering her in the direction of the door.

Daisy twisted away. "Let me go!"

She scanned the room frantically, looking for her bag.

Both nurses stepped towards her, their faces firm.

"Come along now."

"You don't want to make a fuss, do you?"

Daisy spotted her bag lying on the floor by her mum's bed and made a grab for it.

"I brought her all the way from home," she told the nurses, her fingers scrambling to open the buckle. "I have to give her to my mum. I *have* to."

She lifted Dolly Caroline out of the bag, smoothing her hair.

"She saved her once before," Daisy said. "I thought maybe . . . " What *had* she thought exactly? Whatever it was, it suddenly seemed childish, too foolish to put into words.

Both nurses were gazing at her sadly. "Oh, honey . . . " the first one said.

It had been pointless to bring the doll. She was just a thing, like a lampshade was, or a pencil, or an empty coat. But Daisy turned to the bed anyway and placed Dolly Caroline in the crook of her mum's limp arm.

"Look," Daisy said, softly. "She's still wearing her dress and her little shoes. She's still perfect. Please look," she begged. "I brought her for you, Mum."

Her mother didn't move.

Daisy covered her face and burst into tears.

Behind her, one of the nurses gave a little gasp. "Did you see that?" he said.

"What?"

"The right hand. See?"

It might have been the touch of Dolly Caroline's silky hair or the sound of Daisy sobbing. Or perhaps it was both. Caroline Fitzjohn's hand trembled and her breathing deepened. She opened her eyes.

"Daisy?" she said in a faint, astonished voice.

"Who's the doctor on call?" the first nurse asked the other in a high, excited voice. "He needs to be paged *at once*!"

Caroline shifted, struggling to raise her head. "There was an accident," she murmured. "I remember . . . "

"Try not to talk, Mrs. Fitzjohn. The doctor is on his way."

Daisy was still crying, although it was different now. She had never understood how it was possible to cry from happiness. But it was exactly the same as crying from sadness, except you didn't have to try to stop. You could go on crying for as long as you liked.

"How long have I been here?" her mum asked.

"A week," Daisy told her. "And it wasn't an accident. It was Gritting. He came to the house. He tried to hurt me too."

Her mum's eyes widened. "I was so worried. He kept threatening me. He wouldn't stop. I tried to ignore it for as long as I could. Then I knew I had to get help. I was on my way to the police. I was going to tell them about him and about you as well . . . I was going to tell them everything."

"Please don't upset yourself," the nurse urged. Caroline didn't seem to hear. Her eyes filled with tears.

"Oh, Daisy," she whispered. "I've been so wrong for such a long time."

Daisy thought of all the Day Boxes piling up day by day and year by year. Each filled with memories her mum couldn't bear to lose. But some things were meant to be lost.

Perhaps in the end, she thought with a flash of sadness, everything was.

"I want things to be different," Caroline said, her eyes still fixed on Daisy's face.

"You mustn't talk," Daisy told her. "You must rest."

The room was suddenly full of people. A man in a white coat hurried forward and felt her mum's wrist. "Remarkable!" he said, staring at his watch. "Do you have pain anywhere, Mrs. Fitzjohn? How many fingers am I holding up? Can you tell me the name of the current prime minister?"

A nurse drew Daisy aside.

"You must let us do our job now," she said. She led Daisy out of the room into the corridor. Then, much to Daisy's surprise, she suddenly pulled her into a hug. There were tears in her eyes.

"She will get better, won't she?" Daisy asked.

The nurse sniffed and wiped her nose. "It certainly looks like it."

She leaned forward to brush the hair out of Daisy's eyes. "And you'll be just fine as well. To think that nobody knew you were there all that time, alone in that big house!"

Daisy looked at her anxiously. "My mum . . . she won't get into trouble, will she?

The nurse hesitated. "I don't think 'trouble' is the right word," she said. "But I'm not going to lie to you, Daisy. When she gets better, your mum is going to have to answer a lot of questions. People will want to make sure that you are going to be okay. Do you understand?"

Daisy didn't. She was already okay. But it seemed rude to point that out when the nurse was being so kind. So she nodded instead.

"Now let's go to the cafeteria and get some breakfast," the nurse said, straightening up. "You look like you need it. After that, you might like to visit the children's waiting area. There's a lot of fun stuff there. Toys, books, video games. There might even be a couple of other kids to talk to."

Daisy gave her a worried look.

"Trust me," the nurse said, smiling. "I've got a feeling you're going to really like the place."

EIGHT MONTHS LATER

The riverboat was sturdy, built for use rather than beauty. Its hull sat low in the water, and its three snug decks had been weathered by tropical rain and sun until they were the same brown color as the great river itself. The upper deck was open to the sky. From here, it was possible to see in all directions: the vast, slow-moving water ahead and behind, the jungle-smothered banks on either side.

Caroline Fitzjohn had set up her easel in one corner of the deck and was just adding the final touches to a painting of a flock of parrots exploding like fireworks out of the trees. She hesitated for a second, then signed the painting in the bottom right-hand corner and stepped back, staring at it with her head tilted to one side.

"You know, Daisy," her mum said, "if I pluck up all my courage, perhaps I could persuade a gallery to show one or two of my pictures. Maybe one day even an exhibition . . . "

Daisy's mum rubbed the nape of her neck where her hair tickled. It was growing back fast, already a good three inches below the brim of her broad hat.

"Maybe I'm being too ambitious," she added with a flash of doubt.

"No, you're not!" Daisy said. She was sitting cross-legged on the deck with her binoculars around her neck and a notebook on her lap. She was wearing dark green trousers with a lot of pockets and loops, and there was a red bandana tied around her head. She had decided to keep her hair short. It felt light and good that way. "People are going to *love* your pictures," she said.

Her mum stared out across the water at the dark, endless jungle. "I don't know about that," she said. "Although there's something about this place that makes me feel as if all sorts of things are possible." She smiled at Daisy. "I have to admit, when you said you wanted to go to the Amazon, I was a little shocked. Of all the places in the world to go! But you were right. After everything that's happened, it feels perfect."

Her mum paused. "Why *did* you want to come here?"

"I've told you fifty times already," Daisy said. "I made a kind of promise . . . "

"Yes, but a promise to whom?"

"It's hard to explain—" Daisy began, then broke off abruptly. She seized her binoculars and scanned a clump of trees on the right bank. "I thought so!" she cried, recognizing a dark, motionless shape hanging from a branch. "It's a sloth! My first sloth! I can see its face!"

She reached for her notebook. She was making a list of all the animals she had spotted. The list was already fairly long:

pink river dolphin
scarlet macaw (x6)
tamarin monkey (x50?)
piranha (!)
Amazon river turtle
unidentified beetle (large with horns)
anaconda (although it might have been a
   twisty branch)
tapir

"And that's just what I've seen today!" Daisy said, adding *sloth* to the list.

"It's nearly time for supper," her mum said, turning back to her painting. "I should clear this up for the day."

Daisy kept her binoculars trained on the riverbank. She was hoping to catch sight of a jaguar, although she knew it was unlikely because jaguars were extremely rare. The jungle grew right to the edge of the water, so thick it looked impenetrable. But here and there, the roots of particularly large trees had forced small, mud-filled clearings in the otherwise unbroken line of vegetation.

The boat was drawing parallel to one such clearing now. It was just the sort of a place a jaguar might come down to the water to drink.

There were shadows in the clearing, black and white against the deep green trees. Daisy squinted and adjusted the focus on her binoculars. The shadows separated into two figures.

One was a man in a strange helmet with his trousers rolled up to his knees. He was paddling in the muddy water, carelessly, not looking where he put his feet. All of a sudden, he lost his balance. Daisy watched him teeter, arms flailing wildly, then land on his backside with a splash.

The other figure was smaller. She stood high up on the bank, her hands on her hips, her body stiff with exasperation.

Daisy knew exactly what she was saying.

You have any idea how fast piranhas can strip a body to the bone?

Daisy raised her arm to wave. But they were too far away and too busy arguing to see her. Another moment and they were gone, lost in the flow of the swiftly moving river.

"What have you seen?" her mum called. "Another sloth?"

"No, nothing like that."

"What, then?"

Can I be perfectly honest? Daisy thought, smiling a little to herself. She shook her head.

"Just imagining things," she said, jumping up to help her mum with supper.

ACKNOWLEDGMENTS

This book may very well have remained no more than a collection of false starts and muddled drafts without the almost magical guidance and advice of my agent, Rebecca Carter. It is hard to be both kind as well as right, but somehow she manages it. Thanks also to Krestyna Lypen at Algonquin, whose shrewd, tireless editing turned a manuscript into a book, and Anne Sibbald, for her wisdom and support.

Last, but never, ever least, my love and thanks to David Thaler.

D. E. THALER

Tania Unsworth spent her childhood in Cambridge, UK, before moving to America in her early twenties. She currently lives in Boston with her husband and two sons. She's written one previous novel for young readers, *The One Safe Place*. You can find her online at taniaunsworth.com or on Twitter: @TaniaUnsworth1.